# JACK HIGGINS

# A FINE NIGHT FOR DYING

HarperCollins*Publishers*

HarperCollins*Publishers*
77–85 Fulham Palace Road,
Hammersmith, London W6 8JB

www.harpercollins.co.uk

This paperback edition 2003
1

First published (under the name Martin Fallon)
by John Long 1969

First published in paperback by Arrow 1977

Copyright © Martin Fallon 1969

Jack Higgins asserts the moral right to
be identified as the author of this work

ISBN-13: 978-0-00-780909-7

Set in Sabon by Palimpsest Book Production Limited,
Polmont, Stirlingshire

Printed in the UK by CPI Bookmarque, Croydon, CR0 4TD

## PUBLISHER'S NOTE

A FINE NIGHT FOR DYING was first published in the UK by J. Long, London, in 1969 under the authorship of Martin Fallon. The author was, in fact, the writer familiar to modern readers as Jack Higgins. Martin Fallon was one of the names he used during his early writing days. The book was later published in paperback by Arrow – under the authorship of Jack Higgins – but it has been out of print for several years.

In 2003, it seemed to the author and his publishers that it was a pity to leave such a good story languishing on his shelves. So we are delighted to be able to bring back A FINE NIGHT FOR DYING for the pleasure of the vast majority of us who never had a chance to read the earlier editions.

# ENGLISH CHANNEL

## 1969

# 1

There were times when Jean Mercier wondered what life was all about and this was very definitely one of them. Somewhere beyond the boat in the darkness was a shoreline that he could not see, hazards at which he could only guess, and the lack of navigation lights wasn't helping.

A wind that came all the way from the Urals spilled out across the Golfe de St-Malo, driving the waves into whitecaps, scattering spray against the windscreen of the launch. Mercier throttled back the engine and adjusted his steering slightly, straining his eyes into the darkness, waiting for a light like some sign from heaven.

He rolled a cigarette awkwardly with one hand, aware of a trembling in the fingers that would not be stilled. He was cold and tired and very scared, but the money was good, cash on the barrel and tax-free – more than he could earn from three months of fishing. With an ailing wife on his hands, a man had to take what came and be thankful.

A light flashed three times, and then was gone so quickly that for a moment he wondered whether he had imagined it. He ran a hand wearily across his eyes and it flickered again. He watched through a third repetition, mesmerized, then pulled himself together and stamped on the floor of the wheelhouse. There were steps on the companionway, and Jacaud appeared.

He had been drinking again and the smell, sourly sharp on the clean salt air, made Mercier feel slightly sick. Jacaud shoved him to one side and took the wheel.

'Where is it?' he growled.

The light answered him, ahead and slightly to port. He nodded, pushed up speed and turned the wheel. As the launch rushed into the darkness, he took a half-bottle of rum from his pocket, swallowed what was left and tossed the empty bottle through the open door. In the light from the binnacle, he seemed disembodied, a head that floated in the darkness, a macabre joke. It was the face of an animal, a brute that walked on two legs with small pig-eyes, flattened nose and features coarsened by years of drink and disease.

Mercier shuddered involuntarily, as he had done many times before, and Jacaud grinned. 'Frightened, aren't you, little man?' Mercier didn't reply and Jacaud grabbed him by the hair, one hand still on the wheel, and pulled him close. Mercier cried out in pain and Jacaud laughed again. 'Stay frightened, that's how I like it. Now go and get the dinghy ready.'

With a heave, he sent him out through the open door and Mercier grabbed at the rail to save himself. There were tears of rage and frustration in his eyes as he felt his way along the deck in the darkness and dropped to one knee beside the rubber dinghy. He took a spring knife from one pocket, feeling for the line that lashed the dinghy into place. He sawed through it, then touched the razor edge of the blade of his thumb, thinking of Jacaud. One good thrust was all it would take, but even at the thought his bowels contracted in a spasm of fear, and he hastily closed the knife, got to his feet and waited at the rail.

The launch rushed into the darkness and the light flashed again. As Jacaud cut the engine, they slowed and started to drift broadside-on to the beach marked by the phosphorescence of the surf a hundred yards away. Mercier threw the anchor over as Jacaud joined him. The big man heaved the dinghy into the water on his own and pulled it in by handline.

'Off with you,' he said impatiently. 'I want to get out of here.'

Water slopped in the bottom of the dinghy, cold and uncomfortable, as Mercier mounted the two wooden oars and pulled away. He was afraid again, as he always was these days, for the beach was unknown territory in spite of the fact that he had visited it in identical circumstances at least half-a-dozen times before. But there was always the feeling that, this time, things might be different – that the police could be waiting. That he might be drifting into a five-year jail sentence.

The dinghy suddenly lifted on a wave, poised for a moment, then dropped in across a line of creamy surf, sliding to a halt as she touched shingle. Mercier shipped his oars, slipped out and pulled her round, prow facing out to sea. As he straightened, a light pierced the darkness, dazzling him momentarily.

He raised a hand defensively; the light was extinguished, and a calm voice said in French, 'You're late. Let's get moving.'

It was the Englishman again; Rossiter. Mercier could tell by the accent, although his French was almost perfect. The only man he had ever known Jacaud touch his cap to. In the darkness he was only a shadow, and so was the man with him. They spoke together briefly in English, a language Mercier did not understand, then the other man stepped into the dinghy and crouched in the prow. Mercier followed him, unshipping the oars, and Rossiter pushed the boat out over the first wave and scrambled across the bow.

Jacaud was waiting at the stern rail when they reached the launch, his cigar glowing faintly in the darkness. The passenger went up first and Rossiter followed with his suitcase. By the time Mercier had reached the deck, the Englishman and the passenger had gone below. Jacaud helped him to get the dinghy over the side, left him to lash it to the deck and went into the wheelhouse. A moment later, the engines rumbled softly and they moved out to sea.

Mercier finished his task and went forward to make sure that all was secure. Rossiter had joined Jacaud in the wheelhouse and they stood together at the wheel, the Englishman's thin, ascetic face contrasting strongly with Jacaud's – opposite sides of the coin. One an animal, the other a gentleman, and yet they seemed to get on with each other so well, something Mercier could never understand.

As he moved past the wheelhouse, Jacaud spoke in a low voice and they both burst into laughter. Even in that, they were different, the Englishman's lively chuckle mingling strangely with Jacaud's throaty growl, and yet somehow they complemented each other.

Mercier shuddered and went below to the galley.

For most of the way the passage was surprisingly smooth, considering what the Channel could be like at times, but towards dawn it started to rain. Mercier was at the wheel, and as they started the run-in to the English coast, fog rolled to meet them in a solid wall. He stamped on the deck, and after a while Jacaud appeared. He looked terrible, eyes swollen and bloodshot from lack of sleep, face grey and spongy.

'Now what?'

Mercier nodded towards the fog. 'It doesn't look too good.'

'How far out are we?'

'Six or seven miles.'

Jacaud nodded and pulled him out of the way. 'Okay – leave it to me.'

Rossiter appeared in the doorway. 'Trouble?'

Jacaud shook his head. 'Nothing I can't handle.'

Rossiter went to the rail. He stood there, face expressionless, and yet a small muscle twitched in his right cheek, a sure sign of stress. He turned and, brushing past Mercier, went below.

Mercier pulled up the collar of his reefer jacket, thrust his hands into his pockets and stood in the prow. In the grey light of early dawn the launch looked even more decrepit than usual and exactly what it was supposed to be – a poor man's fishing boat, lobster pots piled untidily in the stern beside the rubber dinghy, nets draped across the engine-room housing. Moisture beaded everything in the light rain and then they were enveloped by the fog, grey tendrils brushing against Mercier's face, cold and clammy, unclean, like the touch of the dead.

And the fear was there again, so much so that his limbs trembled and his stomach contracted painfully. He wiped his mouth with the back of one hand and started to roll a cigarette, fighting to keep his fingers still.

The launch slipped through a grey curtain into clear water, and the cigarette paper fluttered to the deck as Mercier leaned forward, clutching at the rail. Two hundred yards away through the cold morning a sleek grey shape moved to cut across their course.

Jacaud was already reducing speed as Rossiter appeared on deck. He ran to the rail and stood there, one hand shielding his eyes from the rain. A signal flashed through the grey morning and he turned, face grim.

'They're saying "Heave to, I wish to board you." It's a Royal Navy motor torpedo-boat. Let's get out of here.'

Mercier clutched at his sleeve, panic rising to choke him. 'Those things can do thirty-five knots, monsieur. We don't stand a chance.'

Rossiter grabbed him by the throat. 'Seven years, that's what you'll get if they catch us with him on board. Now get out of my way.'

He nodded to Jacaud, ran along the deck and disappeared below. The engines roared as Jacaud gave them full throttle, spinning the wheel at the same time, and the launch heeled over, almost coming to a dead stop, then surged forward into the fog.

The grey walls moved in, hiding them from sight, and the door to the companionway banged open and Rossiter appeared with the passenger. He was a black man of middle years, tall and handsome, and wore a heavy overcoat with a fur collar. He looked around in bewilderment and Rossiter spoke to him in English. The man nodded and moved forward to the rail and Rossiter pulled out an automatic pistol and struck him a heavy blow at the base of the skull. The man lurched to one side and fell to the deck without a cry.

What happened next was like something out of a nightmare. The Englishman moved with incredible speed and energy. He grabbed a heavy chain from the stern deck and wound it around the man's body several times. He gave it a final turn about the neck and hooked the two loose ends together with a spring link.

He turned and shouted to Mercier above the roaring of the engine, 'Okay, grab his feet and over with him.'

Mercier stood there as if turned to stone. Without hesitation, Rossiter dropped to one knee and heaved the man into a sitting position. The man raised his head painfully; the eyelids flickered, then opened. He glared at Mercier, not in supplication, but in hate; his lips parted and he cried out in English. Rossiter stooped and manoeuvred him across his shoulders, then straightened and the man went over the rail, headfirst into the sea, and disappeared instantly.

Rossiter turned and struck Mercier heavily in the face, sending him sprawling to the deck.

'Now pick yourself up and get to work on those nets or I'll send you after him.'

He went into the wheelhouse. Mercier lay there for a moment, then got to his feet and stumbled along to the stern. It couldn't have happened. Oh, God, but it couldn't have happened. The deck slanted suddenly as Jacaud spun the wheel again, and Mercier fell on his face in the pile of stinking nets and started to vomit.

It was the fog that saved them, spreading out halfway across the Channel, shrouding them from view on the run back to the French coast.

In the wheelhouse, Jacaud swallowed rum from the bottle Rossiter passed and chuckled harshly. 'We've lost them.'

'Your luck is good,' Rossiter said. 'You must live right.'

'Pity about the package.'

'That's life.' Rossiter seemed completely unconcerned and nodded to where Mercier crouched by the nets, head in hands. 'What about him?'

'A worm,' Jacaud said. 'No backbone. Maybe he should go for a swim, too.'

'And what would you tell them in Ste-Denise?' Rossiter shook his head. 'Leave it to me.'

He went along the deck and stood over Mercier with the rum bottle. 'You'd better have a drink.'

Mercier raised his head slowly. His skin was like the belly of a fish, the eyes full of pain. 'He was still alive, monsieur. Still alive when you put him into the water.'

Rossiter's pale flaxen hair glinted in the early morning sun, making him look strangely age-less. He stared down at Mercier, his face full of concern. He sighed heavily, crouched and produced an exquisite Madonna from one of his pockets. It was perhaps eight inches long and obviously extremely old, carved by some master in ivory the colour of his hair, chased with silver. When he pressed her feet with his thumb, six inches of blue steel appeared as if by magic, sharp as a razor on both edges, honed with loving care.

Rossiter kissed the Madonna reverently, with-out even a trace of mockery, then stroked the blade against his right cheek.

'You have a wife, Mercier,' he said gently,

and his face never lost its peculiarly saintly expression for a moment. 'An invalid, I understand?'

'Monsieur?' Mercier said in a whisper, and the heart seemed to stop inside him.

'One word, Mercier, the slightest whisper, and I cut her throat. You follow me?'

Mercier turned away, stomach heaving, and started to be sick again. Rossiter stood up and walked along the deck and stood in the entrance of the wheelhouse.

'All right?' Jacaud demanded.

'Naturally.' Rossiter took a deep breath of fresh salt air and smiled. 'A fine morning, Jacaud, a beautiful morning. And to think one could still be in bed and missing all this.'

# 2

Fog rolled in across the city, and somewhere in the distance ships hooted mournfully to each other as they negotiated the lower reaches of the Thames on the way out to sea. Fog – real fog of the kind that you seemed to get in London and nowhere else on earth. Fog that killed off the aged, choked the streets and reduced one of the world's great cities to chaos and confusion.

Paul Chavasse abandoned his taxi at Marble Arch and whistled softly to himself as he turned up the collar of his trenchcoat and passed through the gates of the park. There was only one thing he liked better than fog and that was rain. An idiosyncrasy with its roots somewhere in youth, he supposed, or perhaps there was a simpler explanation. After all, both rain and fog enclosed one in a small private world, which could be very convenient at times.

He paused to light a cigarette, a tall handsome man with a face as Gallic as the Pigalle on a Saturday night, and the heritage of his Breton father was plain to see in the Celtic cheekbones. A park keeper drifted out of the shadows and faded without a word, a thing which, considering the circumstances, could only have happened in England. Chavasse went on his way, unaccountably cheered.

St Bede's Hospital was on the far side of the park, a Victorian Gothic monstrosity in spite of its worldwide reputation. They were expecting him, and when he called at Reception, a porter in a neat blue uniform escorted him along a series of green-tiled corridors, each one of which seemed to stretch into infinity.

He was handed over to a senior lab technician in a small glass office, who took him down to the mortuary in a surprisingly modern lift. Chavasse was conscious of two things the moment the doors opened – the all-pervading smell of antiseptic so peculiar to hospitals, and the extreme cold. The vast echoing chamber was lined with steel drawers, each one presumably holding a corpse, but the object of his visit waited for him on an operating trolley covered with a rubber sheet.

'We couldn't get him into one of the boxes, worse luck,' the technician explained. 'Too bloated. Stinking like last year's fish, or worse.'

At close quarters, the smell was quite over-powering, in spite of the preventive measures which had obviously been taken. Chavasse pulled out a handkerchief and held it to his mouth.

'I see what you mean.'

He had looked on death many times in most of its variations, but this monstrosity was something new. He stared down, a slight frown on his face.

'How long was he in the water?'

'Six or seven weeks.'

'Can you be certain of that?'

'Oh, yes – urine tests, the rate of chemical breakdown and so on. He was Jamaican, by the way, or did you know that?'

'So they told me, but I'd never have guessed.'

The technician nodded. 'Prolonged immer-sion in salt-water does funny things to skin pigmentation.'

19

'So it would appear.' Chavasse stepped back and replaced the handkerchief in his breast pocket. 'Thanks very much. I think I've seen all I need.'

'All right for us to dispose of him now, sir?' the technician enquired as he replaced the sheet.

'I was forgetting.' Chavasse took out his wallet and produced a printed disposal slip. 'Cremation only, and all documents to the Home Office by tomorrow.'

'They'd been hoping to have him in the Medical School for dissection.'

'Tell them to try Burke and Hare.' Chavasse pulled on his gloves. 'Ashes to ashes for this boy, and no funny business. I'll see myself out.'

When he had gone, the technician lit a cigarette, a slight frown on his face. He wondered about Chavasse. There was a foreign look about him, but he was obviously English. A nice enough bloke – a gentleman, to use an old-fashioned word, but something wasn't quite right. It was the eyes, that was it. Black and completely expressionless. They seemed to look right through you and beyond, as if you weren't there at all. The kind of eyes that

Jap colonel had had, the one in the camp in Siam where the technician had spent the worst three years of his life. A funny bloke, that Jap; one minute full of the milk of human kindness, the next smoking a cigarette without turning a hair, while they flogged some offender to death.

The technician shuddered and unfolded the slip of paper that Chavasse had given him. It was signed by the Home Secretary himself. That did it. He carefully stowed it away in his wallet and pushed the trolley through into the crematorium next door. Exactly three minutes later, he closed the glass door of one of the three special ovens and reached for the switch. Flames appeared as if by magic, and the body, bloated with its own gases, started to burn at once.

The technician lit another cigarette. Professor Henson wouldn't be too pleased, but it was done now, and after all he did have it in writing. He went next door, whistling cheerfully, and made a cup of tea.

\*　　\*　　\*

It was almost two months since Chavasse had
visited the house in St John's Wood, and return-
ing was like coming home again after a long
absence. Not so strange, perhaps, when one
considered the kind of life he had led for the
twelve years he had been an agent of the Bureau,
the little-known section of British Intelligence
that handled the sort of business no one else
seemed to know what to do with.

He went up the steps and pressed the bell
beside the brass plate that carried the legend
*Brown & Co – Importers & Exporters*. The
door was opened almost immediately by a tall
greying man in a blue serge uniform, who posi-
tively beamed a welcome.

'Good to have you back, Mr Chavasse. You're
nice and brown.'

'Glad to be back, George.'

'Mr Mallory's been asking for you, sir. Miss
Frazer's been phoning every few minutes.'

'Nothing new in that, George.'

Chavasse went up the curving Regency stair-
case quickly. Nothing changed. Not a thing.
It was just like it had always been. Lengthy
periods in which damn-all happened, and then

something broke through to the surface and the day needed twenty-seven hours.

When he went into the small outer office at the end of the narrow corridor, Jean Frazer was seated at her desk. She glanced up and removed her heavy reading glasses with a smile that was always a shade warmer for Chavasse than for anyone else.

'Paul, you're looking fine. It's wonderful to see you again.'

She came round the desk, a small heavy-hipped woman of thirty or so, but attractive enough in her own way. Chavasse took her hands and kissed her on the cheek.

'I never did get around to giving you that evening out at the Saddle Room. It's been on my conscience.'

'Oh, I'm sure it has.' There was a look of scepticism on her face. 'You got my message?'

'My flight was delayed, but the messenger was waiting when I got to the flat. I didn't even have time to unpack. I've been to St Bede's and had a look at the corpus delicti or whatever they call it. Most unpleasant. He'd been in the sea rather a long time. Bleached a whiter shade of

23

pale, by the way, which seemed extraordinary considering what you told me about him.'

'Spare me the details.' She flicked the intercom. 'Paul Chavasse is here, Mr Mallory.'

'Send him in.'

The voice was remote and dry and might have been from another world – a world that Chavasse had almost forgotten during his two months' convalescence. A tiny flicker of excitement moved coldly in his stomach as he opened the door and went in.


Mallory hadn't changed in the slightest. The same grey flannel suit from the same very eminent tailor, the same tie from the right school, not an iron-grey hair out of place, the same frosty, remote glance over the top of the spectacles. He couldn't even manage a smile.

'Hello, Paul, nice to see you,' he said, as if he didn't mean a word of it. 'How's the leg?'

'Fine now, sir.'

'No permanent effects?'

'It aches a little in damp weather but they tell me that will wear off after a while.'

24

'You're lucky you've still got two legs to walk around on. Magnum bullets can be nasty-things. How was Alderney?'

Chavasse's English mother lived in retirement on that most delightful of all the Channel Islands and he had spent his convalescence in her capable hands. It occurred to him, with a sense of wonder, that on the previous day at this time he had been picnicking on the white sands of Telegraph Bay; cold chicken and salad and a bottle of Liebfraumilch frosted from the fridge and wrapped in a damp towel, strictly against the rules, but the only way to drink it.

He sighed. 'Nice, sir. Very nice.'

Mallory got straight down to business. 'You've seen the body at St Bede's?'

Chavasse nodded. 'Any idea who he was?'

Mallory reached for a file and opened it. 'A West Indian from Jamaica named Harvey Preston.'

'And how did you manage to find that out?'

'His fingerprints were on record.'

Chavasse shrugged. 'His fingers were swollen like bananas when I saw him.'

'Oh, the lab boys have a technique for dealing with that sort of problem. They take a section of skin and shrink it to normal size using chemicals. They arrive at a reasonable facsimile.'

'Somebody went to a lot of trouble over the body of an unknown man washed up after six weeks. Why?'

'In the first place, it didn't happen in quite that way. He was brought up off the bottom in the trawl net of a fishing boat out of Brixham, with about seventy pounds of chain wrapped around him.'

'Murdered, presumably?'

'Death by drowning.'

'A nasty way to go.'

Mallory passed a photo across. 'That's him, taken at his trial at the Bailey in 1967.'

'What was he up for?'

'Robbing a gambling club in Birmingham. The Crown lost, by the way. He was acquitted for lack of evidence. Witnesses failed to come forward, and so on. The usual story.'

'He must have had a lot of pull.'

Mallory helped himself to one of his Turkish cigarettes and leaned back in his seat. 'Harvey

Preston arrived in England in 1938 when he was twenty and joined the Royal Army Service Corps during the Munich crisis. His mother and father followed a few months later, with his younger sister, and Preston fixed them up with a small house in Brixton. He was stationed at Aldershot with a transport regiment as a truck driver. His mother gave birth to another son, whom they named Darcy, on the third day of the war in September, 1939. A week later Harvey's regiment was posted to France. During the big retreat when the Panzers broke through in 1940, his unit was badly knocked about and he was shot twice in the right leg. He made it out through Dunkirk and back to England, but was so badly lamed by his wounds that he was discharged with a pension.'

'What did he do then?'

'At first he drove an ambulance, but then he underwent the kind of personal tragedy so common during the Blitz. The house in Brixton took a direct hit during a raid and the only survivor was his young brother. From then on, things seem to have taken a different turn.'

'What did he do?'

27

'Take your pick. Black market, prostitution. After the war he ran a number of illegal gaming clubs and became something of a power in the underworld. Moved into organized crime about nineteen-fifty-nine. The police were certain he was behind a very efficient hijacking organization, but could never prove anything. There were several payroll robberies as well and he was very definitely involved in drug trafficking.'

'Quite a character. What happened after his acquittal? Was he deported?'

Mallory shook his head. 'He'd been here too long for that. But the Yard really turned the heat on. He lost his gaming licence for a start, which put him out of the casino business. It seems they breathed down his neck so hard that he hardly dared stir from his house. It was the money from the Birmingham casino robbery they were after. Even if he couldn't be tried again, they could stop him spending it.'

'Was he married?'

'No, lived on his own. A different girl a night by all accounts, right up to the end.'

A FINE NIGHT FOR DYING

'What about the brother, the one who survived the bombing?'

'Young Darcy?' Mallory actually grinned. 'Funny thing happened there. Harvey kept the boy with him. Sent him to St Paul's as a day-boy. Must have been an extraordinary life for him. Mixing with the sons of the upper crust during the day and the worst villains in London by night. He decided to go in for the law, of all things, passed his bar finals three years ago. Cleared off to Jamaica after Harvey's trial.'

'And what did Harvey do?'

'Left the country on a plane to Rome two months ago. They just about took him to pieces at the airport, but there wasn't a thing on him. They had to let him go.'

'Where did he go from Rome?'

'Interpol had him followed to Naples, where he dropped out of sight.'

'To re-emerge two months later in the bottom of a fishing net off the English coast. Intriguing. What do you think he was playing at?'

'I should have thought that was obvious.' Mallory shrugged. 'He was trying to get into the country illegally. As long as the police didn't

29

know he was here, he could recover his money at leisure and leave by the same way he came, whatever that was.'

Chavasse was beginning to see a little light. 'Someone put him over the side in the Channel, that's what you're suggesting?'

'Something like that. There's a lot of money in this passage-by-night business since the Commonwealth Immigration Act. Pakistanis, Indians, West Indians, Australians – anyone who can't get a visa in the usual way. There's good money in it.'

'There was a case in the paper the other day,' Chavasse said. 'The navy stopped an old launch off Felixstowe and found thirty-two Pakistanis on board. That's a fair night's work for someone.'

'Amateurs,' Mallory said. 'Most of them don't stand a chance. It's the professionals who're getting away with it, the people with the organization. There's a pipeline running all the way through from Naples. The Italian police have been doing some checking and they've come up with an interesting report on a boat called the *Anya* that makes the Naples – Marseille run regularly under a Panamanian registration.'

Chavasse reached for the file, turned it round and went through the photos it contained. There were several of Harvey Preston taken through the years, one on the steps of the Old Bailey after his trial, an arm around the shoulders of his young brother. Chavasse leafed through the reports, then glanced up.

'This is police work. Where do we come in?'

'The Special Branch at Scotland Yard have asked us to help. They feel this job requires the kind of talents more appropriate to one of our operatives.'

'The last time they asked for help, it involved me spending six months in three of the worst jails in Britain,' Chavasse said, 'plus the fact that I nearly got my leg blown off. Why can't they do their own dirty work?'

'We've worked out a suitable background for you,' Mallory said impassively. 'Use your own name, no reason not to. Australian citizen of French extraction. Wanted in Sydney for armed robbery.' He pushed a folder across. 'Everything you need is in there, including a newspaper clipping confirming your criminal background. Naturally, you're willing to pay any price to get into Britain, and no questions asked.'

Chavasse felt, as usual, as if some great sea was washing over him. 'When do I go?'

'There's a three-thirty flight to Rome. You should make it with quarter of an hour to spare if you leave now. You'll find a suitcase waiting for you outside. I had one brought over. A good job you didn't have time to unpack.' He stood up and held out his hand. 'The best of luck, Paul. Keep in touch in the usual way.'

Mallory sat down, replaced his glasses and reached for a file. Chavasse picked up his folder, turned and went out. He was chuckling when he closed the door.

'What's so funny?' Jean Frazer demanded.

He leaned across her desk and chucked her under the chin. 'Prettiest-looking Sheila I've clapped eyes on since I left Sydney,' he said, in a very fair Australian twang.

She stared at him in amazement. 'Are you mad?'

He picked up his suitcase and laughed. 'I must be, Jean. I really must be,' he said, and went out.

# NAPLES – MARSEILLE

# 3

The woman was an Indian and very young – no more than sixteen, if Chavasse was any judge. She had a pale, flawless complexion and sad brown eyes that were set off to perfection by her scarlet sari. Chavasse had seen her only once during the two-day voyage from Naples and presumed they were bound for the same eventual destination.

He was leaning against the rail when she came along the deck. She nodded a trifle uncertainly and knocked on the door of the captain's cabin. It opened after a moment or so, and Skiros appeared. He was stripped to the waist and badly needed a shave, but he smiled ingratiatingly, managing to look even more repulsive than usual, and stepped to one side.

The girl hesitated fractionally, then moved in.

Skiros glanced across at Chavasse, winked and closed the door, which didn't look too good for Miss India. Chavasse shrugged; it was no skin off his nose, he had other things to think about. He lit a cigarette and moved towards the stern of the old steamer.

Pavlo Skiros had been born of indeterminate parentage in Constantinople forty-seven years earlier. There was some Greek in him, a little Turk, and quite a lot of Russian, and he was a disgrace to all three countries. He had followed the sea all his life and yet his right to a master's ticket was uncertain, to say the least. But he possessed other, darker qualities in abundance that suited the owners of the *Anya* perfectly.

He sat on the edge of the table in his small cluttered cabin and scratched his left armpit, lust in his soul when he looked at the girl.

'What can I do for you?' he asked in English.

'My money,' she told him. 'You said you would return it when we reached port.'

'All in good time, my dear. We dock in half

an hour and you'll have to keep out of the way until the customs men have finished.'

'There will be trouble?' she asked in alarm.

He shook his head. 'No trouble, I promise you. It is all arranged. You'll be on your way within a couple of hours.'

He got up and moved close enough for her to smell him. 'You've nothing to worry about. I'll handle everything personally.'

He put a hand on her arm and she drew back slightly. 'Thank you – thank you very much. I will go and change now. I don't suppose a sari would be very practical on the Marseille waterfront at night.'

She opened the door and paused, looking towards Chavasse. 'Who is that man?'

'Just a passenger – an Australian.'

'I see.' She appeared to hesitate. 'Is he another like myself?'

'No, nothing like that.' He wiped sweat from his face with the back of a hand. 'You'd better go to your cabin now and stay there. I'll come for you later when everything is quiet.'

She smiled again, looking younger than ever.

'Thank you. You've no idea what this means to me.'

The door closed behind her. Skiros stood staring at it blankly for a moment, then reached for the bottle of whisky on the table and a dirty tin mug. As he drank, he thought about the girl and what he would do with her when things were nice and quiet and they were alone. The expression on his face was not pleasant.

They reached Marseille on the evening tide and it was already dark when they docked. Chavasse had gone down to his cabin earlier and lay on the bunk, smoking and staring up at the ceiling, on which the peeling paint made a series of interesting patterns.

But then the whole boat left a great deal to be desired. The food was barely edible, the blankets were dirty and the general appearance of the crew, from Skiros down, was pretty grim.

Using the information obtained by the Italian police, Chavasse had approached Skiros in a certain café on the Naples waterfront, flashing a roll of fivers that had set the good captain's eyes gleaming. Chavasse had not used the criminal background part of his story – he had preferred to allow Skiros to discover that for himself. He had simply posed as an Australian anxious to get into the Old Country but denied a visa, and Skiros had swallowed the story. For the money, Chavasse would be taken to Marseille, landed illegally and sent on his way to people who would see him safely across the Channel.

Once on board, he had deliberately left his wallet around, minus his bank roll, but containing, amongst other things, the bogus clipping from the *Sydney Morning Herald* which spoke of the police search for Paul Chavasse, wanted for questioning in connection with a series of armed robberies. There was even a photo, to make certain, and the bait must have been taken, for the cabin had been searched – Chavasse had ways of knowing things like that.

He was surprised he had got this far without some attempt to relieve him of his cash and drop him overboard, for Skiros looked like the kind of man who would have cheerfully sold his sister in the marketplace on very reasonable terms.

Chavasse had slept with the door double-bolted each night and his Smith & Wesson handy under the pillow. He took it out now, checking each round carefully. As he replaced it in the special holster that fitted snugly against the small of his back, there was a knock at the door, and Melos, the wall-eyed Cypriot first mate, looked in.

'Captain Skiros is ready for you now.'

'Good on you, sport.' Chavasse picked up a black trenchcoat and reached for his suitcase. 'It's me for the open road.'

Outside it was raining and he followed Melos along the slippery deck to the captain's cabin. When they went in Skiros was seated at his table, eating his evening meal.

'So, Mr Chavasse, we arrive safely.'

'Looks like it, sport,' Chavasse said cheerfully. 'Let's see now, I gave you five hundred in Naples. That's another five I owe you.'

He produced the roll of fivers and counted a hundred out on the table. Skiros gathered them up. 'Nice to do business with you.'

'Where do I go from here?' Chavasse demanded.

'There is no watchman on this dock. No one will stop you when you pass through the gate. Catch the 9:30 express for Paris. Wait at the bookstall on the platform at the other end and you will be approached by a man who will ask you if you are his cousin Charles from Marseille. Everything is arranged from then on.'

'That's it, then.' Chavasse still kept the bonhomie going as he pulled on his trenchcoat and picked up the suitcase. 'Didn't I see an Indian girl about the place?'

'What about her?' Skiros demanded, his smile fading.

'Nothing special. Just thought she might be on the same kick as me.'

'You are mistaken.' Skiros rose to his feet, wiped his moustache and held out his hand. 'I would not delay, if I were you. You've just got time to catch that train.'

Chavasse smiled at both of them. 'Can't afford to miss that, can I? That would really throw a spanner into the works.'

He went out into the rain, moved along the deck and descended the gangway. At the bottom he paused under the lamp for a moment, then moved into darkness.

Melos turned enquiringly to Skiros. 'A great deal of money in that roll.'

Skiros nodded. 'Get after him. Take Andrew with you. The two of you should be enough.'

'What if he kicks up a fuss?'

'How can he? He's in the country illegally and the Sydney police want him for armed robbery. Use your intelligence, Melos.'

Melos went out. Skiros continued to eat, working his way through the meal methodically. When he had finished, he poured himself a very large whisky, which he drank slowly.

When he went out, the rain was falling more heavily, drifting down through the yellow quarterlights in a silver spray. He moved along the deck to the girl's cabin, knocked and went in.

She turned from the bunk to face him, looking strangely alien in a blue sweater and pleated grey skirt. There was something close to alarm on her face, but she made a visible effort and smiled.

'Captain Skiros. It is time, then?'

'Most certainly it is,' Skiros said and, moving with astonishing speed, he pushed her back across the bunk and flung himself on top of her, a hand across her mouth to stifle any sound.

Melos and the deckhand, Andrew, hurried along the dock and paused by the iron gates to listen. There was no sound, and Melos frowned.

'What's happened to him?'

He took a single anxious step forward and Chavasse moved out of the shadows, turned him round and raised a knee into his groin. Melos sagged to the wet cobbles and Chavasse grinned across the writhing body at Andrew.

'What kept you?'

Andrew moved in fast, the knife in his right hand glinting in the rain. His feet were kicked expertly from beneath him and he hit the cobbles. He started to get up and Chavasse seized his right wrist, then twisted the arm around and up in a direction it was never intended to go. Andrew screamed as a muscle ripped in his shoulder, and Chavasse ran him headfirst into the railings of the gate.

Melos had managed to regain his feet and was being very sick. Chavasse stepped over Andrew and grabbed him by the shirt. 'Was I really being met at that station bookstall in Paris?'

Melos shook his head.

'And the Indian girl? What's Skiros playing at there?'

Melos didn't answer. Chavasse pushed him away in disgust, turned and ran back towards the ship.

The girl's teeth fastened on the edge of the captain's hand, biting clean to the bone. He gave a grunt of pain and slapped her across the face.

'By God, I'll teach you,' he said. 'You'll crawl before I'm through with you.'

As he advanced, face contorted, the door swung open and Chavasse stepped in. He held the Smith & Wesson negligently in one hand, but the eyes were very dark in the white devil's face. Skiros swung round and Chavasse shook his head.

'You really are a bastard, aren't you, Skiros?'

Skiros took a step forward and Chavasse slashed him across the face with the barrel of the gun, drawing blood. Skiros fell back across the bunk and the girl ran to Chavasse, who put an arm around her.

'Don't tell me, let me guess. You're trying to get to England, but they won't give you a visa.'

'That's right,' she said in astonishment.

'We're in the same boat, then. How much did he charge you?'

'He took all my money in Naples. He said he would keep it safe for me.'

'Did he, now?' Chavasse pulled Skiros up and shoved him towards the door. 'Get your case and wait for me at the gangway. The good captain and I have things to discuss.'

When he pushed Skiros through the door of his own cabin, the captain turned angrily, blood on his face. 'You won't get away with this.'

Chavasse hit him across the face with the gun twice, knocking him to the floor. He squatted beside him and said pleasantly, 'Get the girl's money, I haven't got much time.'

Skiros produced a key from his trouser pocket,

dragged himself to a small safe beside his bunk and opened it. He took out a bundle of notes and tossed them across.

'You can do better than that.'

Chavasse pushed him to one side, reached into the safe and picked up a black cashbox. He turned it upside-down and three bundles of notes flopped to the floor. He stuffed them into his pocket and grinned.

'There's a lesson in this for you somewhere, Skiros, and worth every penny.' He tapped him on the forehead with the barrel of the Smith & Wesson. 'And now the address – the real address where we can catch a boat for the Channel crossing.'

'Go to Ste-Denise on the Brittany coast near the Golfe de St-Malo,' Skiros croaked. 'St-Brieuc is the nearest big town. There's an inn called the Running Man. Ask for Jacaud.'

'If you're lying, I'll be back,' Chavasse said.

Skiros could barely whisper. 'It's the truth, and you can do what the hell you like. I'll have my day.'

Chavasse pushed him back against the wall, stood up and went out. The girl was waiting anxiously at the head of the gangway. She had a scarf around her head and wore a plastic mac.

'I was beginning to get worried,' she said in her soft, slightly sing-song voice.

'No need.' He handed her the bundle of notes he had taken from Skiros. 'Yours, I think.'

She looked up at him in a kind of wonder. 'Who are you?'

'A friend,' he said gently, and picked up her suitcase. 'Now let's get moving. I think it would be healthier in the long run.'

He took her arm and they went down the gangway together.

# FRANCE

# 4

They caught the night express to Brest with only ten minutes to spare. It wasn't particularly crowded. Chavasse managed to find them an empty second-class compartment near the rear, left the girl in charge and ran to the station buffet. He returned with coffee, sandwiches and half-a-dozen oranges.

The girl drank some of the coffee gratefully, but shook her head when he offered her a sandwich 'I couldn't eat a thing.'

'It's going to be a long night,' he said. 'I'll save you some for later.'

The train started to move and she stood up and went into the corridor, looking out over the lights of Marseille. When she finally turned and came back into the compartment, a lot of the strain seemed to have left her face.

'Feeling better now?' he asked.

'I felt sure that something would go wrong; that Captain Skiros might reappear.'

'A bad dream,' he said. 'You can forget it now.'

'Life seems to have been all bad dreams for some time.'

'Why not tell me about it?'

She seemed strangely shy, and when she spoke, it was hesitantly at first. Her name was Famia Nadeem and he had been wrong about her age. She was nineteen, and had been born in Bombay. Her mother had died in childbirth and her father had emigrated to England, leaving her in the care of her grandmother. Things had gone well for him, for he now owned a thriving Indian restaurant in Manchester and had sent for her to join him three months earlier after the death of the old woman.

But there had been snags of a kind with which Chavasse was only too familiar. Under the terms of the Immigration Act, only genuine family dependants of Commonwealth citizens already in residence in Britain could be admitted without a work permit. In Famia's case, there was no formal birth certificate to prove her identity conclusively. Unfortunately, there had been a great many false claims and the authorities were now sticking rigorously to the letter of the law. No absolute proof of the claimed relationship meant no entry, and Famia had been sent back to India on the next flight.

But her father had not given up. He had sent her money and details of an underground organization which specialized in helping people in her predicament. She was disconcertingly naïve, and Chavasse found little difficulty in extracting the information he required, starting with the export firm in Bombay where her trip had commenced, passing through Cairo and Beirut, and culminating in Naples with the agents who controlled the *Anya*.

'But why did you give Skiros all your money?' he said.

'He said it would be safer. That there were those who might take advantage of me.'

'And you believed him?'

'He seemed kind.'

She leaned back in her seat, head turned to look through her own reflection into the darkness outside. And she was beautiful – too beautiful for her own good, Chavasse decided. A lovely vulnerable young girl on her own in a nightmare world.

She turned and, catching him watching her, coloured faintly. 'And you, Mr Chavasse? What about you?'

He gave her his background story, cutting out the criminal bit. He was an artist from Sydney who wanted to spend a few months in England, which meant working for his keep, and there was a long, long waiting list for permits. He wasn't prepared to join the queue.

She accepted his story completely and without any kind of query, which was bad, considering that it was so shot full of holes. She leaned back again and gradually her eyes closed. He reached for his trenchcoat and covered her. He was beginning to feel some kind of responsibility, which was really quite absurd. She was nothing to him – nothing at all. In any case, with any kind of luck, things would go through pretty smoothly once they reached Ste-Denise.

But what would happen when they arrived

on the English coast and Mallory acted on his information? She'd be on her way back to Bombay for good. They'd never allow her into the country again after an attempt at illegal entry. Life could be very difficult at times. Chavasse sighed, folded his arms and tried to get some sleep.

They reached St-Brieuc just before five o'clock in the morning. The girl had slept peacefully throughout the night and Chavasse awakened her just before they arrived. She disappeared along the corridor, and when she returned, her hair was combed neatly into place.

'Any hot water down there?' he asked.

She shook her head. 'I prefer cold in the morning. It freshens you up.'

Chavasse ran a hand over the hard stubble on his chin and shook his head. 'I'm not too fond of being skinned alive. I'll shave later.'

The train glided into St-Brieuc five minutes later. They were the only passengers to alight. It was cold and desolate and touched with that atmosphere peculiar to railway stations the world over in the early hours of the morning. It was as if everyone had just left.

The ticket-collector, well protected against the chill morning air by a heavy overcoat and scarf, looked ready for retirement. He seemed indifferent to everything, even life itself, and the pallor of his skin, coupled with his constant, repetitive coughing, boded ill. He answered Chavasse with a kind of frigid civility, as if his attention was elsewhere.

Ste-Denise? Yes, there was a bus to Dinard which would drop them within a mile of Ste-Denise. It left at nine o'clock from the square. They would find a café there which opened early for the market people. Monsieur Pinaud was not one to miss trade. He subsided once more into his own cheerless world, and they moved on.

Rain drifted across the square as they went down the steps and crossed to the lighted windows of the café. It was warm inside, but not busy. Chavasse left the girl at a table by the window and moved to the zinc-topped bar.

A middle-aged balding man in striped shirt and white apron, presumably the Monsieur Pinaud referred to by the ticket-collector, was reading a newspaper. He pushed it to one side and smiled. 'Just off the train?'

'That's it.' Chavasse ordered coffee and rolls. 'They tell me there's a bus to Dinard at nine o'clock. That's definitely the earliest?'

Pinaud nodded as he poured the coffee. 'You want to go to Dinard?'

'No, Ste-Denise.'

The coffee-pot froze in mid-air and the man glanced across warily. 'Ste-Denise? You want to go to Ste-Denise?'

His reaction was more than interesting and Chavasse smiled amiably. 'That's right. My girl-friend and I are spending a few days' holiday there. I've arranged to stay at an inn called the Running Man with a Monsieur Jacaud. You know him?'

'Perhaps, monsieur. A lot of people come in here.' He pushed the coffee and rolls across.

Chavasse took the two cups and the plate of rolls across to the table. As he sat down, Pinaud wiped the zinc top of the bar carefully, then moved to a door which obviously led to the rear, and vanished.

'I'll only be a minute,' Chavasse told the girl, and went after him.

He found himself in a deserted, stone-flagged corridor. A notice at the far end indicated the lavatory. There was no sign of Pinaud. Chavasse started forward cautiously and paused. A door on his right was slightly ajar. From the sound of it, Pinaud was on the telephone. The interesting thing was that he was speaking in Breton, which Chavasse, whose paternal grandfather still presided over the family farm near Vaux in spite of his eighty years, spoke himself like a native.

'Hello, Jacaud. Those two packages you were expecting have arrived. The girl fits the description perfectly, but the man worries me. Speaks French like a Frenchman, or like a Frenchman should, if you follow me. Yes – okay. They're waiting for the bus at nine.'

Chavasse slipped back into the café. Famia was already on her second roll. 'Hurry up,' she said. 'Your coffee will be getting cold.'

'Never mind. I'm just going across to the

station to check on that bus time again. I won't be long.'

He went out into the rain without giving her a chance to reply and hurried across to the station. It was still deserted, but he quickly found what he was looking for, a series of metal lockers, each with its own key, where luggage might be left. He took out his wallet and also the extra money he had taken from Skiros. He pushed the whole lot well to the rear of the locker, closed it quickly and concealed the key beneath the insole of his right shoe.

Famia was looking anxious when he returned to the café. He patted her hand reassuringly and went back to the counter.

'I wondered what had happened to you,' Pinaud said.

Chavasse shrugged. 'I thought there might be a local train or something. It's a hell of a time to wait.'

'Don't worry about that.' Pinaud gave him a big smile. 'You just sit tight and have another coffee. Lots of farmers and market people are in and out of here at this time in the morning. I'll get you a lift to Ste-Denise. Someone is bound to be going that way.'

'Very decent of you. Perhaps you'd join me in a cognac? It's a cold morning.'

'An excellent idea.' Pinaud reached for a bottle and a couple of glasses and filled them quickly. 'Your good health, monsieur.' He raised his glass and smiled.

Chavasse smiled right back. 'And yours.'

The brandy burned all the way down. He picked up his coffee and returned to the table to await events.


People came and went, mainly porters from the nearby market, and Chavasse bought the girl another coffee and waited. It was perhaps half an hour later when the old van turned out of a narrow street on the other side of the square.

He watched idly as it approached, and noticed a Renault emerge from the same street and halt at the kerbside. The van came on and braked no more than a couple of yards from the café window. Jacaud got out.

The girl reacted immediately. 'That man –

what a terrible face. He seems so – so completely evil.'

'Appearances can sometimes be very deceptive,' Chavasse told her.

Jacaud paused just inside the door, glancing casually around the room as if seeking a friend before proceeding to the counter, and yet he had marked them. Chavasse was sure of it. He purchased a packet of cigarettes and Pinaud said something to him. He glanced over his shoulder at Chavasse and the girl then turned away again. Pinaud poured him a cognac and came round the counter.

'You are in luck, monsieur,' he told Chavasse. 'This man is going to Ste-Denise. He has agreed to give you a lift.'

Chavasse turned to the girl and said in English: 'Our good-looking friend has offered us a lift. Should we accept?'

'Is there any reason why we shouldn't?'

He smiled and shook his head. 'You're really very refreshing, but hopelessly out of date. Still – never look a gift horse in the mouth.'

Jacaud swallowed his cognac and crossed to the door. He paused and glanced down at

Chavasse, face expressionless. 'You are going to Ste-Denise, I understand? I'm on my way there now. You're welcome to a lift.'

'Wonderful,' Chavasse said brightly. 'We'll be right with you.'

Jacaud nodded briefly to Pinaud. 'I'll be in touch about further arrangements,' he said in Breton, and went out.

He was already behind the wheel when Chavasse and the girl joined him. There was room for one passenger. The girl took the only seat, and Chavasse heaved the suitcases into the rear and climbed over the tailboard. The van started at once, bouncing its way across the cobbles, passing the parked Renault. He caught a quick glimpse of the driver, a flash of very fair hair, and then the car pulled away from the kerb and came after them, which was interesting.

Chavasse touched the butt of the Smith & Wesson snug in its holster against his spine, then sat back and waited to see what was going to happen.

\*    \*    \*

Within a few minutes, they had left the town and were travelling along a narrow country road. The heavy rain and a slight ground mist reduced visibility considerably, but he caught an occasional glimpse of the sea in the distance beyond a fringe of pine trees.

The Renault stayed so close that he could see the driver clearly, a pale man with extraordinary fair hair who looked more like a priest than anything else. They came to a crossroads at a place where the pinewoods seemed to move in on every side. The van carried straight on, the Renault turned left and disappeared. Chavasse frowned.

The van swerved into a narrow sandy track to the left and moved down through the pine trees towards the sea. A few moments later, the engine coughed a couple of times, faltered, then cut out completely. They rolled to a halt, the door opened and Jacaud came round to the rear.

'Trouble?' Chavasse enquired.

'I've run out of petrol,' Jacaud said. 'But it doesn't matter. I always carry an emergency supply. At the back of the bench there.'

Chavasse found an old British Army jerrycan

that looked as if it had been in use since Dunkirk. It was full, which made it awkward to handle in the confined space, and he had to use both hands, which was obviously exactly what Jacaud had counted on. As Chavasse heaved the jerrycan up on the tailboard with every sign of difficulty, the big man's hand appeared from behind his back and the tyre lever he was holding cracked down.

Only Chavasse wasn't there any longer. He dodged to one side, holding the jerrycan in both hands with negligent ease, and the tyre lever dented the edge of the tailboard. Jacaud was already moving backwards out of harm's way, every instinct that had kept him intact for forty-three years warning him that he had made a very bad mistake, but he was too late. The jerrycan took him full in the chest and he went over. He rolled on his face and started to get up and Chavasse landed on his back.

The arm that clamped itself around Jacaud's throat was like a steel band, cutting off his air supply so efficiently that he started to choke at once.

Chavasse wasn't really sure what happened

64

after that. He was aware of Famia screaming, calling his name, and then the light was switched off very suddenly. There was no pain – no pain at all. A blow to the base of the neck delivered by an expert – the thought was there and yet was not there, and in the same moment vision returned.

He looked up into the face of a ravaged saint, an Anthony burned clear to the bone by the heat of the wilderness. Beneath the drift of flaxen hair the pale blue eyes were empty. There was no love here, no cruelty either, and he crouched beside Chavasse in a kind of meditation, an exquisite ivory Madonna clasped in both hands.

Chavasse was aware of the Smith & Wesson hard against his back, secure in its spring holster. Famia Nadeem stood beside the van, hands together, terror on her face, and Jacaud stood beside her. Chavasse decided to play it cool for another couple of minutes. He came back to Rossiter, stared at him vacantly and ran a hand across his eyes.

The Englishman slapped him in the face. 'Can you hear me, Chavasse?' Chavasse struggled up on one elbow, and Rossiter smiled briefly. 'I was

65

beginning to think I must have hit you harder than I had intended.'

'Hard enough.' Chavasse sat up, rubbing the nape of his neck with one hand. 'You've heard from Skiros, I presume?'

'Naturally. He gives me to understand that you have in your possession a considerable sum of money belonging to the organization I work for. Where is it?'

'In a safe place back in St-Brieuc. I decided it would make what a poker player might term a good ace-in-the-hole. Who am I talking to, by the way? You're not Jacaud, that's for sure.'

'Monsieur Jacaud you have already met. My name is Rossiter.'

'And he and Skiros work for you?'

'In a manner of speaking.'

'Then I don't think much of the way your organization treats its cash customers. When I reached Marseilles, Skiros sent me on my way to the wrong destination with a couple of goons on my tail to rob me. When I went back to the ship to talk things over, he was doing his best to rape the girl. On top of that, he'd taken her for a lot of money. I don't know how well he's been doing for you, but I'd say his bank account would make interesting reading.'

Rossiter didn't seem to be listening. He had turned to Famia Nadeem, a frown on his face. When he went forward, she glanced down and he put a hand under her chin and tilted it up.

'Is he telling the truth?'

Strangely enough, all her fear seemed to have vanished. She looked up at him calmly and nodded. Rossiter turned abruptly and came back to Chavasse. His eyes were bleak and there was an expression of utter desolation on his face.

'What a world,' he said softly. 'What a filthy, loathsome world.' He took a deep breath, something clicked and he was himself again. 'Get up!'

Chavasse did as he was told, producing the Smith & Wesson at the same time. Jacaud gave a kind of angry cry, but Rossiter waved him to silence. He stood, feet slightly apart, tossing the ivory Madonna high into the air and catching it again in his right hand.

'Now what?'

'Now nothing,' Chavasse said. 'I just want to get to London in one piece and fade into the background.'

67

'Understandable enough.' Rossiter actually smiled. 'Ten years in an Australian jail can hardly have been an exciting prospect. I believe they still run their penal system on rather old-fashioned lines.'

Chavasse managed to look suitably astonished. 'Is there anything you don't know, sport?'

'Not where clients are concerned.'

Chavasse sighed and put the Smith & Wesson away. 'I've had my bellyful of trouble during the past few months, Rossiter. I don't want any more. Just get me to England, that's all I ask. I'll pay whatever is necessary. That business in Marseille was all Skiros, believe me.'

Rossiter slipped the Madonna into his right pocket. 'The money? Where is it?'

Chavasse told him. He also took off his right shoe and produced the key, which Rossiter immediately tossed to Jacaud. 'We'll wait for you here. You can take the Renault.'

Jacaud moved away through the trees without a word and Chavasse lit a cigarette. So far so good. He looked down through the pine trees towards the sea, and smiled.

'Nice country. I was looking forward to this

68

bit of the trip. My father came from Brittany, you know.'

'I was wondering about your French,' Rossiter said. 'It's really quite excellent.'

'My mother was English, of course, but we've never used anything else but French in the house since I can remember. My old man wouldn't have it any other way.'

Rossiter nodded, produced a slim leather case from his breast pocket and selected a thin black cheroot, which he lit carefully. 'Tell me something about the girl.'

She was sitting in the passenger seat, watching them. Chavasse threw her a smile. 'I only know what she's told me.'

He went through her story quickly, and when he had finished, Rossiter nodded briefly. 'She's very young to have gone through so much.'

He said it as if he meant it, with real sympathy in his voice, and moved towards her. Chavasse sat down on a fallen log and watched them. Rossiter was speaking, the girl answered. Suddenly she was smiling, and a few moments later, laughed out loud. And Rossiter laughed with her, that was the strangest thing of all, so

that for a short time he seemed to be an entirely
different person. Curiouser and curiouser . . .

Chavasse gave up for the moment, got to his
feet and walked to the edge of the clearing,
breathing in the scent of damp pines, the good
salt air from the sea, the smell that always
brought the Brittany of his boyhood back to
him, wherever he was. It would have been nice
to have surprised his grandfather at Vaux. The
old man would have loved that – an unexpected
visit from his clever half-English grandson who
lectured at a university whose name he could
never remember. A little bit too much of the
scholar with his doctorate in modern languages,
but still a Chavasse for all that.

Chavasse stared down through the trees
towards the sea remembering boyhood a thousand years ago and all its wonderful dreams.
And now he had returned to Brittany and he
could not go to Vaux . . .

A horn sounded through the trees. Jacaud
had arrived, and he sighed and came back to
the present as Rossiter called to him.

# BRITTANY

# 5

Ste-Denise was twenty or thirty granite cottages amongst pine trees fringing a horseshoe cove that was a natural harbour. There was a wooden jetty of sorts, with an old thirty-foot launch moored to it that looked as if it had seen better days. The tide was turning, and four clinker-built fishing cobles moved out to sea in line astern. A similar boat lay stranded on the beach above the high water mark and two men worked on her hull.

Chavasse took it all in as the van moved out of the trees along the narrow road that merged into the High Street of the village. The only sign of life was a stray dog sitting mournfully in the rain outside a cottage door.

The van left the village behind, and almost stalled as Jacaud dropped two gears to negotiate a steep hill. The Running Man was at the top, a two-storeyed granite house sheltering behind high walls. Jacaud turned through an archway and halted in the cobbled courtyard inside. Chavasse got out and looked around with interest. The whole place had a strangely forlorn look about it and badly needed a coat of paint. A shutter banged to and fro in the wind, and when he glanced up, a curtain moved slightly at a window, as if it had been pulled to one side while someone glanced out.

The Renault entered the courtyard and pulled up just behind the van. Famia got out and stood there, looking uncertain. Rossiter came round from the other side, picked up her suitcase and took her elbow. She looked tired, ready to drop at any moment. He leaned over her solicitously, murmured something and took her inside.

Chavasse turned to Jacaud. 'What about me?'

'If I had my way, you could sleep in the pig-sty.'

'Careful,' Chavasse said. 'You'll be making sounds like a man next. Now let's try again.'

Jacaud went inside without a word and Chavasse picked up his suitcase and followed him. He paused to glance up at the painted sign above the door. It was obviously very old and showed a man running, apparently some kind of fugitive, a pack of hounds at his heels. A pleasant sight indeed, the terror in the poor wretch's eyes frozen into place for all eternity.

Inside was a large square room with a low-beamed ceiling and a tiled floor. There was a scattering of chairs and tables, a large open hearth in which a fire burned, and a marble-topped bar.

Jacaud had gone behind it and was pouring himself a large cognac. He rammed the cork into the bottle and Chavasse dropped his case. 'I'll join you.'

'Like hell you will. Let's see the colour of your money.'

'Rossiter's got it all, you know that.'

'Then you can go thirsty.' He replaced the bottle on the shelf and raised his voice. 'Hey, Mercier, where are you?'

A door at the back of the bar opened and a small, worried-looking man of forty or so came in. He wore a fisherman's patched trousers and was wiping his hands on a grimy towel.

'Yes, monsieur, what is it?'

'Another passenger for the *Leopard*. Take him upstairs. He can share with Jones.'

He glared at Chavasse like some wild animal, turned, kicked open the door and vanished into the kitchen.

'Quite a show,' Chavasse said. 'Is he always like this or is today something special?'

Mercier picked up the suitcase. 'This way, monsieur.'

They mounted some stairs to the first floor and moved along a narrow whitewashed corridor past several doors. Mercier knocked on the one at the far end. There was no reply and he opened it.

The room was small and bare, with whitewashed walls, two narrow truckle beds standing side by side. There was a crucifix on one wall, a cheap colour reproduction of St Francis on the other. It was clean – but only just.

Mercier put down the case. 'Monsieur Jones will probably be back shortly. He is, by the way, Jamaican. A meal will be served at twelve-thirty. If there is anything else you wish to know, you must see Monsieur Rossiter.'

'And who does Monsieur Rossiter have to see?'

Mercier frowned, looking genuinely bewildered. 'I don't understand, monsieur.'

'Let it go,' Chavasse told him.

Mercier shrugged and went out. Chavasse put his suitcase on one of the beds, moved to the window and looked out. So this was the Running Man? Not a very prepossessing sight.

Behind him, someone said, 'Welcome to Liberty Hall, man.'


A gull cried high in the sky and skimmed the sand dunes. Down by the water's edge, Jones threw stones into the sea. He turned and moved back towards Chavasse, tall, handsome, the strong angular face and startling blue eyes evidence of that mixture of blood so common in the West Indies. *Jack Jones?* Well, that was as reasonable a name as any. He had the shoulders of a prizefighter and looked good for ten rounds any day of the week, or Chavasse was no judge.

He flung himself down on the sand, produced

a packet of Gauloises and lit one. 'So you're from Australia?'

'That's it – Sydney.'

'They tell me that's quite a town.'

'The best. You should try it some time.'

The Jamaican stared at him blankly. 'You must be joking. They wouldn't even let me off the boat. They like their immigrants to be the pale variety, or hadn't you noticed?'

It was a plain statement of fact, without any kind of rancour in it, and Chavasse shrugged. 'I don't make the laws, sport. Too busy breaking them.'

The Jamaican was immediately interested. 'Now that explains a lot. I was wondering why a free, white, upstanding Protestant like you was having to use the back door into the old country like the rest of us.'

'Catholic,' Chavasse said. 'Free, white, upstanding Catholic – just for the record.'

Jones grinned, produced his packet of Gauloises for the second time and offered him one. 'And just how badly does the law back home want you?'

'About ten years' worth. That's if I'm lucky

and the judge isn't feeling too liverish on the great day.'

Jones whistled softly. 'Man, you must be a real tiger when you get going.'

'A weakness for other people's money, that's my trouble.' Chavasse looked across the sand dunes to the small harbour and the sea beyond. 'This is all right; about the nicest beach I've touched since Bondi.'

'That's what I thought five days ago – now it's just a drag. I want to get moving.'

'What are you going to do when you get over the Channel?'

Jones shrugged. 'I've got friends in the right places. They'll fix me up with something.'

'But for how long?'

'As long as I need. Once I hit London, I can't go wrong. I'll just merge into the scenery. After all, one black face is the same as another, or hadn't you noticed?'

Chavasse refused to be drawn. 'What about the rest of the clientele?'

'If you turn your head a couple of points to starboard, you'll see them now.'

The old man who appeared over a sand dune

a few yards away wore a blue overcoat two sizes too large that gave him a strangely shrunken look, and his brown, wrinkled skin was drawn tightly over the bones of his face. He wasn't too steady on his feet, either. Chavasse got the distinct impression that if it hadn't been for the woman who supported him with a hand under his left elbow and an arm around his shoulders, he might well have fallen down.

'Old Hamid is seventy-two,' Jones said. 'A Pakistani. He's hoping to join his son in Bradford.'

'And the woman?'

'Mrs Campbell? Anglo-Indian – a half-and-half. What they used to call chi-chi in the good old days of Empire. A fine Scots name, but she can no more get away from the colour of her skin than I can. Her husband died last year and her only relative is a sister who married an English doctor years ago and went to live in Harrogate, of all places. Mrs Campbell tried to get an entry permit to join her, but they turned her down.'

'Why?'

'She doesn't qualify as a dependant under

the Immigration Act, she's an Indian national and she's got tuberculosis. She was born in India, never been to England in her life and yet she talks about it as going home. Funny, isn't it?'

'Not particularly.'

Mrs Campbell was about fifty, with sad dark eyes and a skin that was darker than usually found amongst Eurasians. She seemed cold and wore a shabby fur coat, a heavy woollen scarf wrapped about her neck and head.

They paused, the old man gasping for breath. 'A cold day, Mr Jones, don't you agree?'

Jones and Chavasse stood up and Jones nodded. 'This is Mr Chavasse, a new arrival. He'll be going with us.'

The old man showed no surprise. 'Ah, yes, Miss Nadeem spoke of you.'

'You've met her?' Chavasse said.

'Just before we left for our walk,' Mrs Campbell put in.

Hamid held out a soft, boneless hand, which Chavasse touched briefly before it slipped from his grasp as easily as life would slip from the frail old body before very much longer.

Mrs Campbell seemed curiously embarrassed and tugged at the old man's sleeve. 'Come now, Mr Hamid, we mustn't dawdle. Lunch soon. So nice, Mr Chavasse.' Her English was quaint in its preciseness, and the way in which she spoke was an echo of a bygone age. Chavasse watched them stumble away across the sand dunes, strange, shadowy creatures with no substance to them, adrift in an alien world, and was conscious of an indescribable feeling of bitterness. Men made laws to protect themselves, but someone always suffered – always.

He turned and found Jones watching him enigmatically. 'You look sorry for them, too sorry for any Sydney duck with the law on his tail.'

There was a curious stillness between them. Chavasse said in a harsh, unemotional voice, 'I don't know what in the hell you're talking about.'

'Neither do I, man.' Jones grinned, and the moment passed. 'You want to eat, we'd better move.'

They made their way through the sand dunes and started across the beach above the wooden jetty. Chavasse pointed towards the motor launch moored beside it. 'Is that the boat?'

Jones nodded. 'It kind of fits in with Jacaud, wouldn't you say?'

'What do you make of him?'

Jones shrugged. 'He'd sell his sister or his grandmother for a bottle of rum at the right time. He's on two a day at the moment and escalating.'

'And the man who works for him – Mercier?'

'Frightened of his own shadow. Lives in a cottage on the other side of the village. Just him and his wife. She's some kind of an invalid. A walking vegetable. He jumps when Jacaud roars.'

'And Rossiter?'

Jones smiled softly. 'You like the question bit, don't you?'

Chavasse shrugged. 'Suit yourself.'

'Okay, I will. You know what a zombie is?'

Chavasse frowned. 'Something to do with voodoo, isn't it?'

'To be precise, a dead man brought out of his grave before corruption's had a chance to set in.'

'And given life, is that what you're trying to say?'

'A kind of life, to walk the night and do his master's bidding – a creature of pure, mindless evil.'

'And that's Rossiter.'

'That's Rossiter.' The Jamaican laughed harshly. 'The funny thing is, he used to be a priest – a Jesuit priest.'

'And how would you know that?'

'Ran out of matches one night, so I knocked on his door. He didn't seem to be around.'

'And your natural curiosity got the better of you?'

'What else, man? There were a couple of interesting photographs in the bottom right-hand drawer of his dressing table. He hasn't changed much. There's a nice one dated 1949 of about twenty of them in a group – looks like graduation day at the seminary. The other was taken in 1951 in Korea. Shows him with half-a-dozen kids at the gate of some mission or other.'

*Nineteen-fifty-one. The year the Korean War had started*. Was that where Rossiter had lost his faith? Chavasse frowned, remembering that tortured, ascetic face. The priest he could see,

but the murderer . . . it just didn't seem possible.

He was still thinking about it as they turned
into the courtyard of the Running Man.

# ENGLISH CHANNEL

# 6

The main room of the inn was deserted when they entered, and Jones went behind the bar and took down a bottle of cognac and two glasses from the shelf.

'Join me?' he said.

Chavasse nodded. 'Why not?'

There was a sudden bellow of anger as Jacaud appeared through the rear door. 'Put those down. You hear me, you black ape?'

Jones looked him over calmly, not a flicker of emotion on his face. 'Sure I hear you,' he observed, in very reasonable French.

He uncorked the bottle and filled both glasses. Jacaud took a quick step towards him, grabbed him by the shoulder and spun him around.

'Jacaud!' Rossiter spoke from the doorway, his voice full of steel, brooking no denial.

Jacaud turned reluctantly. 'They don't even pay,' he muttered lamely.

Rossiter ignored him and came forward. He was wearing grey trousers, a hand-knitted fisherman's sweater and steel-rimmed spectacles. He carried a slim book in one hand, a finger marking his place.

'Be my guests, gentlemen.'

'Are you going to join us?' Chavasse enquired.

'Mr Rossiter don't drink,' Jones said. 'We're on our own, man.'

He saluted Chavasse, emptied his glass in a single swallow and filled it again. Jacaud, scowling, took down a bottle and glass for himself and retired to the other end of the bar.

'You've been for a walk, I see,' Rossiter said.

Chavasse nodded. 'That's right. It's quite a spot. They must do well in the tourist season round here.'

'Too far off the beaten track and they don't encourage strangers.'

'I was wondering when we make our move.'

'I can't be certain. We have one more passenger. It depends when he arrives. It could be today or tomorrow.'

'And what's the form when we do go?'

'You'll be told at the appropriate time. No need to worry. We know what we're doing.'

Behind them a soft voice said hesitatingly, 'May I come in?'

Famia stood in the doorway, her flawless complexion set off to perfection by a scarlet sari. There was a silver rope necklace about her neck, gold bracelets on her wrists. It was the reactions of his companions that interested Chavasse most. Jones was giving her the kind of appraisal you saw on the face of a connoisseur in an art gallery when confronted with something of value. Jacaud gazed at her with ill-concealed lust. And Rossiter? Rossiter seemed transfixed. His face had turned very pale, which made the eyes seem bluer than ever, and then a strange thing happened. He smiled, and it was as if something had melted inside.

He went forward and gave her his arm. 'They should be ready for us. Shall we go in?' he said, and took her through into the dining room.

He had left his book on the bar counter and Chavasse picked it up. It was the Everyman edition of *The City of God* by St Augustine.

There were times when Chavasse got the distinct impression that he was the only sane person in a world gone mad. This was very definitely one of them. He emptied his glass, nodded to Jones, and went after them.

There was a large walled garden behind the inn, a sad sort of place with gnarled apple trees long since run to seed from lack of proper attention. There were no flowers as yet, for it was still too early in the season and last year's grass overflowed onto the narrow paths, still uncut.

Famia walked there, Rossiter at her side, a figure from Brueghel in her scarlet sari, vivid against that grey-green landscape. She laughed, and the sound rose on the quiet air to the window of Chavasse's room, where he sat with Jones, watching from behind the curtain.

'First time I've seen him smile,' the Jamaican said.

'She's certainly touched something,' Chavasse replied. 'But I'm not sure what.'

Rossiter murmured to the girl, turned and went away. She walked on by herself, pausing to look up at a blackbird on a branch above her head. A moment later, Jacaud appeared.

He was obviously drunk, and swayed slightly as he moved forward, staring at her unwinkingly. She failed to see him, still intent on the blackbird, until he reached out and touched her shoulder. She turned, recoiling immediately, but he caught her by the arm, pulled her close and kissed her. Perhaps he meant no more than that, for as she cried out, struggling to be free, he laughed.

Jones beat Chavasse to the door by a short head. They went down the stairs, along the passage and out through the kitchen. Already they were too late.

Rossiter stood halfway between them and Jacaud, an arm around the girl. Very gently, he put her to one side, his hand slipped into his pocket and came out holding the ivory Madonna.

Jacaud didn't even try to escape, that was the strangest thing of all. He fell on his knees, his great face working as Rossiter slowly advanced, grabbed the Breton by the hair and pulled back his head. There was a sharp click, and steel flashed. Very deliberately, Rossiter drew the point of the razor-sharp blade across Jacaud's forehead; the flesh opened and blood oozed in a crimson curtain.

Jacaud rolled over without a sound and Rossiter wiped the knife mechanically. Famia stood looking at him, a dazed expression on her face. He went to the girl, put an arm around her shoulders and led her past Chavasse and Jones without a glance.

Chavasse turned Jacaud over and dropped to one knee. He took out his handkerchief and wiped the blood away from the great ugly face.

'How is he?' Jones asked.

'Fainted dead away – fright, I expect. Rossiter knew what he was doing. He's marked him badly – no more than that. Sticking plaster should be enough.'

'Did you see his face?'

'Rossiter's?' Chavasse nodded. 'Reminded me of something in Marlowe's play *Faustus*.'

'This is hell, nor am I out of it?' Jones said. 'More than apt.'

Chavasse grinned. 'One thing about the

Jamaican educational system – they certainly
must have encouraged you to read.'

'And write, man. And write. Hell, it's the
coming thing.'

The Jamaican got a shoulder under Jacaud's
arm and raised him. Together they took him
inside.

Later in the afternoon, the rain came again
with a sudden rush, shrouding everything in
a grey curtain. The old woman who did the
cooking came in from the kitchen and lit an
oil lamp, retiring immediately without a word.
Mrs Campbell and Hamid sat as close to the fire
as possible and talked quietly with Famia. Jones
was reading a book, and Chavasse sat with a
week-old copy of *Le Monde*.

He dropped it to the floor and went to the
door which led to the bar. Rossiter and Jacaud
sat at a table, talking in low tones, a bottle of
cognac between them. Otherwise the place was
empty, except for Mercier, who stood behind
the bar counter polishing glasses. It seemed as
good an opportunity as Chavasse was ever likely

to get, and he turned, strolled across the room and went into the passage.

He went up the stairs two at a time, moved along the corridor and paused outside Rossiter's room. The lock was child's play, an old mortice that opened smoothly with the first skeleton key he tried, and he went inside.

The room was almost exactly the same as his own, small and bare, with a single bed and an old chest of drawers. It was a place of shadows with the grey light of late afternoon seeping in through the narrow window, but two tall candles burning steadily on either side of a statue of the Virgin gave all the additional illumination that he needed.

There was a suitcase under the bed that contained nothing but clothes. He replaced them neatly and pushed it out of sight again. He went through the drawers next and found the photographs Jones had mentioned, exactly as described. Chavasse examined them in the flickering light of the candles and Rossiter's face jumped out to meet him, clear and quite unmistakable.

He replaced them carefully and searched the other drawers. There was nothing more of interest, which left only the books standing in a neat row on the window ledge. The Bible, a *Life of St Ignatius Loyola*, *The City of God* and various commentaries. There were also copies of *The Sayings of Chairman Mao* and *Das Kapital*, which certainly made for a most Catholic collection in more senses than one.

He checked that everything was as he had found it, opened the door cautiously and stepped out. Jones moved from the shadows of an alcove almost immediately opposite, and smiled.

'Was I right?' he demanded coolly.

Chavasse nodded. 'On the nose.'

'The story of my life. I'm right so often, it's sickening.'

There was the sound of a car pulling up outside. They moved to the window at the end of the passage and peered out. A Mercedes was parked at the entrance and Rossiter and Jacaud stood beside it. Jacaud opened the rear door and a man emerged, wearing a heavy overcoat with an astrakhan collar and a black, old-fashioned trilby. He was Chinese and built like a fort, with a round, smooth, enigmatic face that made his age difficult to judge.

'Man, this gets more like the United Nations every minute,' Jones whispered.

Chavasse nodded, as the Mercedes drove away and Jacaud picked up the newcomer's bags. 'The other passenger, presumably. We'd better get down and see what the form is.'

In the living room Rossiter was already making introductions, and when Chavasse and Jones appeared, he turned with a pleasant smile. 'Ah, now we are all here. Gentlemen, Mr Cheung.'

The Chinese came forward to shake hands. Close up, he was perhaps forty-five, with a smile of exceptional charm. 'So, an Australian?' he said to Chavasse. 'I have had many dealings with firms in your country. I am from Hong Kong.'

He shook hands with Jones rather formally and with considerably less enthusiasm, and then disappeared with Rossiter and Jacaud, who at close quarters looked white and ill, a great strip of surgical tape pasted across his brow.

'At least he shook hands,' Jones observed. 'They don't like my kind of people, man, or did you know that already?'

'To the Chinese, a person of any other race is

naturally inferior,' Chavasse said. 'So don't start feeling sorry for yourself. I'm in there too.'

He went out into the passage and helped himself to one of the old oilskins hanging from the wooden pegs. Jones leaned in the doorway and watched him. 'Going somewhere?'

'I feel like some air.'

'Mind if I tag along?'

'Suit yourself.'

The Jamaican took down an oilskin and they went out into the rain. It fell straight from sky to earth, for there was no wind, and when they went out through the archway Ste-Denise was almost hidden from view. Chavasse went down through the pine trees and moved along the beach into the sand dunes, thinking things over.

There was the organization, apparently simple enough in its aims, which were to get you across the Channel and into the UK, no questions asked, for cash on the barrel. Except that they were also willing to put you over the side in chains in the right circumstances. Having met Jacaud and Rossiter, that fact was becoming easier to accept by the minute.

And what about Rossiter? The Jesuit who

had lost his faith, presumably in Korea where a vicious and bloody confrontation with China had dragged on for years. Hamid, Famia and Mrs Campbell were easy enough to accept, and Jones, of course, fitted neatly into place, but Mr Cheung from Hong Kong? Now he really was an interesting piece of the jigsaw.

He paused on top of a sand dune and looked out over the grey sea. Jones nudged him in the ribs. 'You see what I see? They showing the latest customer over the boat.'

Chavasse squatted, pulling Jones down beside him. Rossiter and Cheung were walking along the wooden jetty towards the *Leopard*. As he watched, they scrambled onto the deck and disappeared down the companionway.

'I wonder what they're up to?' Jones said.

'Only one way of finding out.'

Chavasse got to his feet and went down towards the water, keeping to the cover of the sand dunes, and Jones followed him. The small fishing fleet had long since returned from the day's work, and the boats were drawn up on the beach in a neat row that gave excellent cover.

Within a few moments they had reached the

shelter of the jetty. Chavasse paused and Jones said, 'What exactly did you have in mind?'

'God knows – just my curiosity. I'd like to know what they're doing.'

He worked his way along the heavy timbers, climbing to the next level at the point where grey-green water slopped in lazily. The heavy smell of the sea hung over everything, salt-water, seaweed, dead fish, harsh and pungent, but not unpleasant. He crouched in a cross-piece, Jones right behind him. There were footsteps on the deck above their head.

Rossiter and Mr Cheung were talking together in Cantonese. Chavasse strained every nerve to hear what was being said, but could only catch odd words and phrases. There was a sudden burst of laughter and then the footsteps drummed on the boards overhead as they walked away.

'What were they talking about?' Jones said.

Chavasse shook his head. 'I couldn't catch everything. Putting it together, it seems that Cheung has been sent from a place called Hellgate by a man named Montefiore. Does that make any kind of sense to you?'

Jones nodded. 'Montefiore is something new,

but Hellgate I've come across before. I overheard a conversation between Rossiter and Jacaud.'

Chavasse scrambled up the cross-ties and looked down at the deck of the *Leopard*. It was a depressing sight, shabby and uncared for, festooned with nets and cluttered with lobster pots. The rubber dinghy had been inflated and a powerful outboard motor was attached to its stern.

'One thing's certain,' he said. 'If anything goes wrong, some of us will be swimming. That thing won't hold more than four and make progress. Come on, we'd better get out of here.'

They scrambled back along the timbers and reached the beach again. As they moved up through the sand dunes, Jones chuckled.

'What's so funny?' Chavasse asked.

'You are.' Jones contrived to look innocent. 'Man, you're the only Australian I've ever met who could speak French and Chinese as well as English. Those Sydney schools must really be something.'

'You go to hell,' Chavasse said, and moved on through the pine trees towards the inn.

\*       \*       \*

When they entered, Rossiter was standing alone at the bar and Mercier was in the act of pouring him a brandy. The Englishman turned and smiled. 'Ah, there you are. We were looking for you.'

'We felt like a breath of air,' Chavasse said. 'Anything important?'

'I think so. You'll be pleased to know we're leaving tonight at approximately nine o'clock.'

'How long will the crossing take?'

'About seven hours. If the weather holds, you'll be landed on a beach near Weymouth.'

'Will we be met?'

'Naturally. My colleagues on the other side will have you in London by nine a.m. at the latest. After that you are on your own.'

'And what happens if something goes wrong?' Jones said.

Rossiter looked faintly surprised. 'But it never does, I can assure you. I'll see you later.'

He went out, closing the door, and a small, trapped wind scuffled in the corners and died.

Jones sighed. 'Wish I had his confidence. You think this thing is going to work?'

'Do you?' Chavasse said.

They challenged each other, each man's thoughts unspoken. Jones broke first, his face creasing into a smile. 'I know one thing. It's certainly going to be an interesting night.'

# 7

The jetty at night was a lonely place, a lantern on a six-foot pole the sole illumination. In its harsh light, the *Leopard* looked less of a bargain than ever, old and ugly like a whore who has seen better days, caught without her make-up on.

Mercier was there, and Jacaud, working on deck when the party from the Running Man arrived. Rossiter led the way, carrying Famia's suitcase. Where the girl was concerned, he was all solicitude, helping her to the deck and handing her down the companionway. The others followed, Chavasse and Jones taking old Hamid and Mrs Campbell between them in turn.

Rossiter held Chavasse back, a hand on his sleeve. 'A word before you go below.'

'Something troubling you?' Chavasse enquired politely.

'Your gun.' Rossiter held out his hand. 'No nonsense, now. There's a good chap.'

Chavasse shrugged, produced the Smith & Wesson and handed it over. 'You're the boss.'

'For a few hours more. Now let's join the others.' He nodded to Jacaud. 'Any time you're ready.'

Chavasse went down the companionway to the cabin and found the rest of them already seated on either side of a central table, looking absurdly formal, as if it was some kind of board meeting and they were waiting for the chairman. Jones pushed up to make room for him on the padded bench and smiled.

'What kept you?'

Before Chavasse could reply Rossiter appeared. He leaned on the end of the table, his hands taking his weight. 'Ladies and gentlemen, we're about to commence the final leg of your journey. If the weather holds, and I can assure you that the forecast is a favourable one, you will be landed approximately seven hours from now in a creek near a small village not far from

Weymouth on the English coast. A member of our organization will be waiting there to take you on to London by road. For the rest of the voyage, I must ask you to stay in your cabin. Are there any questions?' No one spoke, and he smiled. 'You'll find sandwiches through there in the galley, if anyone feels hungry, and a small stove on which you can make coffee. I'll see you later.'

He left, and almost immediately the engines coughed into life and the boat started to move. Chavasse peered out of the nearest porthole and saw Mercier standing under the lantern on the jetty as the *Leopard* moved out to sea. He walked away and Chavasse sat down again.

Jones offered him a cigarette. 'Well, what do you think now?'

'They seem to know what they're up to.' Chavasse leaned across to Famia. 'Everything okay?'

She smiled brightly. 'Fine, just fine. Mr Rossiter has been so kind. He gives one such a feeling of confidence. I'm sure everything is going to be all right now.'

'Let's hope so.'

Chavasse leaned back. The business with the Smith & Wesson had given him something to think about. There could well be some sinister motive behind it. On the other hand, it was perfectly possible that Rossiter was simply taking every precaution. Not that it mattered, for Chavasse, who had long ago learned by bitter experience never to leave anything to chance, still had his Walther PPK automatic, which before leaving, he had strapped to the inside of his left leg just above the ankle with a piece of surgical tape.

He sat back, eyes half-closed, and watched Cheung, who was reading a book at the far end of the table on the opposite side next to Mrs Campbell. Chavasse wondered what it was, and in the same moment remembered two things: Rossiter's excellent Chinese and the copy of *The Sayings of Chairman Mao* he had seen in his room. Yes, indeed, the more he thought about it, the more interesting Mr Cheung became.

With a love of the sea not unnatural in a man whose Breton ancestors had been voyaging to the coast of Newfoundland to fish long before Columbus had discovered the New World, Chavasse had been running a thirty-foot motor yacht out of Alderney for eight years and knew the Golfe de St-Malo and the general area of the Channel Islands like the back of his hand.

Because of this, he was able to keep a reasonably accurate check on their progress, not only from an estimate of the boat's speed, but by direct observation of various lights which were familiar to him.

Although the weather remained fair, the boat pitched considerably in the turbulence common to the area because of the great tidal surge which drives in through the Channel Islands, raising the level of the water in the Golfe by as much as thirty feet. Both Hamid and Mrs Campbell were suffering from sea-sickness in spite of the pills which Rossiter had handed round at the inn before leaving, and the old man didn't look at all well.

It wasn't just the pitching of the *Leopard* which was causing the trouble. There was an all-pervading stench of petrol, which seemed to have got steadily worse for the last hour.

Chavasse looked out of the porthole as they rounded Les Hanois lighthouse on the western tip of Guernsey.

He told Jones, 'A clear run from here. Shouldn't take more than a couple of hours, if the weather holds.'

Jones made a wry face. 'Much more of this and I'll be sick myself. That petrol sure stinks.'

Chavasse said in a low voice, 'I'm not too happy about it. Think I'll go on deck and have a word with our friend.'

The door at the top of the companionway was locked. He hammered on it with his clenched fist. After a while, it opened and Rossiter peered in.

'What do you want?'

'We're getting one hell of a whiff of petrol down here,' Chavasse told him. 'Old Hamid's been sick several times now. He doesn't look too good.'

Rossiter crouched down and sniffed. A frown appeared on his face. 'I see what you mean. Better bring him up for a breath of air while I get Jacaud to check the engine.'

Jones and Chavasse took the old man up

the companionway between them. There was a fair sea running, and a strength three wind, if Chavasse was any judge, but the old boat was coping nicely. The masthead light swung rhythmically from side to side. Jacaud crouched beside the hatch which gave access to the engine. He disappeared from view, and Chavasse left Jones to look after Hamid and crossed to the open hatch.

There was only four feet of headroom inside, and Jacaud had to squat at the bottom of the short ladder while fumbling for the light switch in the dark. He found it, and in the sudden illumination the trouble was plain enough to see, for an inch or so of petrol slopped around his feet.

He edged forward and disappeared from view, reappearing almost immediately. 'How bad is it?' Chavasse asked, as he came up the ladder.

Jacaud ignored him, replaced the hatch and went to the wheelhouse. Chavasse returned to Jones, who stood at the rail, an arm around Hamid.

'What gives?' Jones demanded.

Chavasse shrugged. 'Jacaud wasn't exactly forthcoming. I'd say he has a leak in the fuel tank.'

'Quite correct.' Rossiter joined them, a match flaring in his cupped hands as he lit a cigarette. 'As it happens, we have auxiliary tanks which carry enough fuel for the entire trip in themselves. Jacaud has switched over to them. I think you'll find that things will improve very quickly now.'

'Do we have to return below?' Chavasse asked.

'One of you can stay up here with the old man for another ten minutes or so. He should be all right again by then.'

He went back into the wheelhouse and Chavasse turned to Jones. 'You okay here?'

'Sure.'

'Good – then I'll go below and see how the others are getting on.'

When he went down the companionway to the saloon, the smell of petrol still lingered, but it was nowhere near as strong as it had been earlier. Mrs Campbell looked pale and wan, but Famia seemed fine, and Cheung leaned back in his seat, eyes closed, hands folded across his chest.

Chavasse glanced out of the porthole above his head. In the distance, the green and red navigation lights of a ship following the steamer lane that ran up-Channel from Ushant disappeared, as if a curtain had dropped into place. He peered out, frowning, and there was a step on the companionway.

Jones eased old Hamid into a seat and grinned. 'Not too good out there now. Mist coming in off the water and it's started to rain again.'

At that precise moment, the boat was rocked by a muffled explosion. Mrs Campbell screamed as she was thrown halfway across the table and Chavasse fetched up against the far wall. As he picked himself up, the *Leopard* came to a dead halt and then started to drift.

Chavasse hammered on the door of the companionway. It opened almost at once and Rossiter peered in, a gun in his hand. His face had turned very pale, the eyes glittered, and yet the gun didn't waver in the slightest.

'Back you go.'

'Don't be a damn' fool,' Chavasse said. 'If there's trouble, we've got a right to know about it.'

'When I'm good and ready.' Rossiter pushed him back and slammed the door.

'What's wrong up there?' Jones demanded. 'It certainly didn't sound too healthy to me.'

In the stress of the moment his accent had undergone a surprising transformation, replaced by the kind of faultless clipped enunciation common to the products of the English public-school system.

Mrs Campbell was sobbing hysterically and Famia was trying to comfort her. Old Hamid seemed to have come to life in some strange way and was on his feet, an arm around both women. It was Cheung's reactions which were the most interesting. No panic, no hysterics. He sat at the table, face expressionless, eyes watchful.

Chavasse unscrewed one of the portholes and peered out. There was a smell of burning, and Rossiter and Jacaud were arguing in French just above his head.

'It's no good, I tell you,' Jacaud cried, and there was panic in his voice. 'The old tub has had it.'

'How far from the coast are we?' Rossiter demanded.

'Five or six miles – maybe seven.'

'Good – we'll continue in the rubber boat. Get it over the side. Our friends at Fixby can run us back to Ste-Denise.'

The rest of the conversation was blown away on the wind and Chavasse turned to face Jones, who knelt on the seat beside him.

'What's going on?' Jones demanded.

'From what they say, the *Leopard*'s had it. They're talking about going the rest of the way in the rubber boat.'

'Can it be done?'

'I don't see why not. It's about six miles to the coast and they've got a good outboard motor on that thing. Of course, there's only room for four passengers, but I shouldn't think that will present much of a problem to Rossiter.'

The door to the companionway was flung open with startling suddenness and Rossiter appeared, the gun in his hand. He waved it at Chavasse and Jones. 'Right, sit down and stay down.'

They did as they were told. Chavasse leaned across the table and groped for the butt of the Walther PPK that was strapped to his leg above the ankle.

Rossiter nodded to Famia. 'All right, Miss Nadeem, on deck.'

She shook her head, complete bewilderment on her face. 'But I don't understand.'

The mask of calmness cracked into a thousand pieces; he grabbed her roughly by the arm and cried wildly, 'You want to die, do you?' He pushed her up the companionway. 'Go on – get on deck.'

Mrs Campbell sagged into her seat as Famia stumbled out of sight, and Chavasse said, 'What do we do? Go down with the ship singing "Abide with me"?'

Rossiter ignored him and spoke to Cheung in rapid Chinese. 'On deck quickly. The boat is sinking.'

The Chinese pushed past Hamid and Mrs Campbell, and Chavasse leaned across the table, his hand fastening around the butt of the Walther. 'I've certainly got to give it to you, Rossiter. It must have taken nerve to see Harvey Preston off the way you did, but this is even better. Four at one go . . .'

Rossiter turned and fired, blindly and in a kind of reflex action, the bullet splintering the bulkhead behind Chavasse and a foot to one side. Mrs Campbell screamed again. Chavasse sent Jones to the floor with a shove in the back and brought the Walther up fast. The bullet caught Cheung on the side of the face, gouging a bloody furrow across one cheek, chipping wood from the doorpost as it went on its way.

Cheung didn't utter a sound. He spun round and flung himself up the companionway, and Rossiter fired three shots wildly. Chavasse went under the table. As the echoes died away, the door was slammed shut and the bolt clicked.

He got to his feet and found Jones already on his way to the companionway. Chavasse got to him just in time and dragged him back as two more shots came through the door.

'Wait, man – wait! He was expecting one of us to do that.'

They flattened themselves against the wall on either side of the companionway, and Jones said softly, 'You know your business, I'll say that for you.'

Chavasse grinned. 'You don't do too badly yourself for a barrister.'

Jones showed no surprise at all. 'You know who I am?'

'Darcy Morgan Preston, aged twenty-nine, profession barrister; in practice in Jamaica since August, 1967. Married, two children. You're trying to find out what happened to your brother Harvey.'

'And you know?'

'Our friends put him over the side, wrapped in about sixty pounds of anchor chain.'

Darcy Preston straightened and moved away from the wall, his face sagging. At the same moment the outboard motor coughed into life outside.

'Let's go,' Chavasse said, and jumped into the companionway.

He fired four times, splintering the wood

around the lock, raised his right foot and stamped hard. The door swung back and he went through to the deck, crouching. He was already too late; the sound of the outboard was fading into the darkness and mist.

# 8

'Nice people,' Darcy Preston said quietly. 'Now what do we do?'

There was a sudden hiss as if gas were escaping, and a cloud of steam billowed from the engine-room hatch. Already the stern was low in the water and the *Leopard* wallowed sluggishly, hardly lifting as the swell undulated across the sea.

There was a sudden exclamation from the companionway, and when Chavasse turned, old Hamid was standing there. In the diffused yellow light from the masthead lamp, he looked about a hundred years old. He didn't seem afraid in the slightest when he spoke.

'They have gone, Mr Chavasse? They have left us to drown?'

'Not if I can help it,' Chavasse told him. 'How's Mrs Campbell?'

'Not too good, I'm afraid.'

Chavasse turned to Preston. 'Get her up on deck and see if you can find some liquor. Jacaud liked his rum, so there must be a few bottles around. Make her drink as much as you possibly can. Anything to calm her down. I'll see what I can find up here. And hurry, for God's sake. We haven't got long.'

He found three lifejackets in a locker in the wheelhouse and passed one to Hamid. The old man started to unbutton his overcoat and Chavasse shook his head.

'Keep that on, whatever you do. It's going to be cold out there.'

The old man pushed his arms through the straps and Chavasse did a final deck check. The only movable item that might support a person's weight was the aft hatch cover. He got it off and eased it towards the rail, as Preston appeared with Mrs Campbell.

She looked ghastly in the yellow light, eyes dark and fearful, her body shrunken with terror. Chavasse could smell the rum. Preston was holding one bottle in his hand and there were two more under his arm.

He passed one across to Chavasse. 'Stick that in your pocket. It might come in useful.'

Chavasse gave him the two lifejackets. 'The best I can do.'

'And what about you?'

'There's an old cork lifebelt here that will keep me going. Now hurry it up. We've only got a few minutes.'

Suddenly it seemed very quiet, the rain falling in dull steel lances through the light, and they stood by the rail together, ready to go. The sea was already over the stern and slopped in across the deck in a green curtain.

Chavasse glanced at his watch. 'Dawn in another hour. We're between five and six miles off the coast, possibly less, but the tide will start to go in fast soon and we'll go with it. Don't try to swim, that way you'll tire quickly and lose body heat, and don't try to take any clothes off. That would be the worst thing you could do. Mrs Campbell, we're going to put you on the hatch. I want you to just lie still, even if the water breaks over you. The rest of us will hang onto the sides. It's important we try to stay together – any questions?'

The *Leopard* gave a sudden lurch to one side, and Preston lost his balance and went into the water. He surfaced and grabbed for the rail. He even managed a smile.

'We should do this more often. Better get the hatch over fast. Somehow I don't think the boat has much longer to live.'

Strange how one always thought of a boat as a living creature with a soul of its own. Swimming awkwardly, the cork lifebelt under his armpits bumping the side of the hatch as he pushed hard, Chavasse glanced back and watched the *Leopard* slide smoothly under the surface. For a brief moment the green and red navigation lights gleamed above the swell at the masthead, and then they too were dimmed.


It was the darkness that was the real enemy, not the cold, though that was bad enough to begin with. But after a while the bodily temperature adapted itself and the fact that they were all fully clothed helped considerably, as Chavasse knew it would.

But the darkness remained for quite some

time, and Mrs Campbell moaned repeatedly, breaking into terrible fits of crying every so often that no one could do anything about.

Gradually, the dawn came with a kind of grey luminosity because of the mist. Visibility was no more than a hundred yards, and Chavasse noticed with some unease the freshening breeze cold on his left cheek and the whitecaps that were starting to appear all about them.

He turned to Hamid, who hung onto the hatch beside him. The old man was well out of the water because of his lifejacket, but his turban was soaked, his skin shrunken so that every bone showed.

'Are you all right? Can you hang on?'

Hamid nodded without replying and Chavasse pulled his way round to the other side to Darcy Preston, who gave him a tired grin.

'Give me Montego Bay any time. This is no joke.'

'The wind is picking up,' Chavasse said. 'Can you feel it? It'll push us inshore that much faster, but things are going to get rough, so watch out.'

Preston's mouth opened in a soundless cry.

Chavasse turned and saw a grey-green wall of water coming in fast, blocking out the sky. There wasn't a thing he could do about it, nothing anyone could do. This time Mrs Campbell, God help her, didn't even get time to scream. The wave lifted the hatch like a cork chip, turned it over and smashed it down.

Chavasse surfaced in a maelstrom of white water, struggling for breath, still buoyant, thanks to the old lifebelt. Mrs Campbell was twenty or thirty feet away, Darcy Preston swimming after her. Hamid was over to the right, and Chavasse kicked out towards him.

The old man looked badly shaken. He had lost his turban and his long iron-grey hair had come loose and floated on the water as he lay back, obviously exhausted. As Chavasse reached him, the wind tore a gap in the curtain of mist and he saw land low down on the horizon, no more than a mile away at most.

So Jacaud had been over-cautious in his estimate? Either that or they had come in a damned sight faster than he had realized. He turned towards Preston, who was still swimming after

Mrs Campbell, and shouted, 'Land! No more than a mile!'

Preston raised an arm to signify that he understood and continued to swim after Mrs Campbell. The curtain of mist dropped back into place. Chavasse reached the old man and pulled him close.

'Not much longer now. I saw land.'

Hamid smiled wanly, but seemed unable to speak. Chavasse got the bottle of rum out of his pocket and pulled the cork with his teeth. 'Drink some of this.'

He forced the old man's mouth open and poured. Hamid coughed, half-choked, and pulled his head away. 'It is against my religion,' he gasped.

Chavasse grinned. 'Allah will forgive you this once, old man,' he said in Urdu, and swallowed the rest of the rum.

Strangely enough, the old man's only reaction to being addressed in his own language was to reply in the same tongue. 'If I live, it is because Allah wills it. If I am to die – so be it.'

\* \* \*

Another half-hour and Chavasse was really beginning to feel the cold. He had taken off the belt of his trenchcoat and had used it to secure himself to Hamid, who floated beside him. There was no sign of Darcy Preston or Mrs Campbell – hadn't been for some time now.

Old Hamid was still, eyes closed, his face a death mask, blue with cold. Chavasse slapped him a couple of times and the eyes opened to stare blankly. A kind of recognition dawned. The lips moved, the words were only a whisper.

'Ali – Ali, is it you, my son?' he asked in Urdu.

'Yes, my father.' It took everything Chavasse had to make the correct reply. 'Not long now. Soon we will be home.'

The old man smiled, his eyes closed and suddenly a wave took them high into a sky of lead, holding them above the water long enough for Chavasse to see cliffs through driving rain no more than a couple of hundred yards away. Between lay wave after wave, and white water crashing in to meet the distant shore.

From that moment they moved fast, helpless

in the grip of the current that carried them with it. Chavasse gripped the old man tightly as water broke over them, and then another great wall of water, green as bottle glass, smashed down on them.

Chavasse went deep, too deep, and found himself alone, fighting for life like a hooked fish. His lifebelt had gone, old Hamid had gone, but strangely, no panic touched him. If he was to die, he would die fighting.

There is a behaviour pattern common to all animals and known to psychologists as the critical reaction, a phrase that describes the fury with which any living creature will fight for survival when there is no other way, either backed into a corner by his enemies or alone in a sea of white water, as Paul Chavasse was now.

He broke surface, sucked air into his lungs and went under again, tearing at the buttons of his trenchcoat. He got it off, and then the jacket, and came up for more air. The shoes took a little longer, probably because his feet were swollen from their long immersion in cold salt-water, but suddenly he was free of those too and swimming again, his rage to live giving him strength drawn from that hidden reserve that lies dormant in every man.

And then his foot kicked sand and he went under again. A wave took him forward across a great rounded boulder streaming with water and he found himself knee-deep in seaweed.

Another wave bowled him over. His fingers hooked across a rib of rock, and he held on as the waters washed over him. As they receded, he staggered to his feet and stumbled across the rocks to the safety of a strip of white sand at the base of the cliffs.

He lay on his face, gasping for air, then forced himself to his feet. Hamid – he had to find Hamid. The sea was in his mouth, his ears, his throat, it seemed to sing inside his head as he turned and picked his way through the rocks to the main beach.

He saw Hamid at once, thirty or forty yards away, lying in the shallows, the water breaking over him. Chavasse started to run, calling out in Urdu, 'I'm coming. Hold on! Hold on!'

Stupid, really. The old man would be dead, he knew that. He dragged the body clear of the water, turned it over and, greatest of all miracles, the old eyes opened.

Hamid smiled, all fatigue and pain washed from his face. 'Ali, my son, I knew you would come,' he whispered. 'Bless me now.'

'You are blessed, old man, hold my hand,' Chavasse said in Urdu. 'Blessed and thrice blessed. Go with Allah.'

The old man smiled contentedly, his eyes closed, and the life went out of him.

Chavasse crouched there beside him for quite a while, unaware of the cold, staring blindly into space. When he finally stood up, Darcy Preston was waiting a few yards away, watching him gravely.

Like Chavasse, he was down to shirt and trousers and his lifejacket had gone. There was a cut on his face, another on his left arm.

'What about Mrs Campbell?' Chavasse asked.

Preston shrugged. 'I tried to catch her when that big wave split us all up, but the current was too strong for me. She was still float-ing when I last saw her. She could still make it.'

Not that he believed that – neither of them

did, and Chavasse said wearily, 'Okay, let's get out of here.'

'Aren't we going to move him?'

'Let's put it like this,' Chavasse said. 'The way things are at the moment, it would make a lot more sense if you and I didn't hang around to be found with him. If we take him higher up the beach, they'll know someone put him there.'

'But what in the hell are we going to do?' Preston demanded.

Chavasse looked at his watch. 'It's a quarter to five. We find the road and the nearest phone box. I put through a call to my people, then we get behind the nearest hedge and wait. You'll be on the way to London in an hour.'

Darcy Preston shook his head. 'Well, one thing's certain. Whatever else you are, you can't be the police.'

'Full marks,' Chavasse said. 'Now let's get out of here,' and he turned and moved towards the cliffs through the grey morning.

# LONDON

# 9

'Montefiore – Enrico Montefiore.' Mallory turned from the window, filling his pipe from an elegant leather pouch. 'One of the richest men in Europe, though very few people have ever heard of him. Doesn't like having his picture taken, but you'll find one or two in his file. He's the kind of big financier who's almost gone out of style. A shadowy figure somewhere in the background, with his finger in so many pies you lose count.'

'And Hellgate?' Chavasse asked. 'What about that?'

Mallory shook his head. 'Doesn't mean a thing. As I recall, Montefiore has a place on Lake Lucerne and a palazzo in Venice. Actually, he's rather dropped out of sight during the past three or four years.' He shook his head. 'This doesn't make any kind of sense at all. Why on earth would a man of Montefiore's background be mixed up in a thing like this?'

There was a knock at the door and Jean Frazer came in. She handed Mallory an envelope. 'More material from S2, sir, courtesy of CIA. China Section.'

She went out and Mallory opened the envelope and took out several record cards, each with a photo pinned to it. 'Better look at these, Paul. See if anyone strikes a chord.'

Cheung was number five, only his name was Ho Tsen and he was a colonel in the Army of the People's Republic of China. It was an excellent likeness and Chavasse passed it across.

'That's our boy.'

Mallory checked through the card and nodded, a slight frown on his face. 'Quite a character. One of their best men, from the looks of this. Rather stupid to pass him off as a Military Attaché in Paris for three years. The CIA was bound to catch on to him.'

The telephone buzzed; he picked it up and listened for just over a minute. When he replaced the receiver, he looked thoughtful.

'That was Travers calling in from this place, Fixby. It's a little village on a creek near Weymouth. There's a broken-down boatyard just outside it run by a man named Gorman. He's missing at the moment. Last seen moving out to sea at about six this morning in a thirty-foot launch he uses to take people big-game fishing.'

Chavasse looked at his watch and saw that it was almost noon. 'They'll be nearly there by now, if the weather holds.'

'Ste-Denise?' Mallory nodded. 'Yes. I'm inclined to agree with you, and our friend from the People's Republic will have returned with them if I'm any judge. For one thing, he's going to need some kind of medical attention, and for another, he won't want to hang around now that things have turned sour. Very practical people, the Chinese.'

'What about Rossiter?'

Mallory picked up a flimsy, and examined it. 'Now he really is an amazing character. I can't get over him. Stoneyhurst, a double first at Cambridge, five years at the English College in Rome and then Korea. The Chinese had him

137

for four years – four years behind the wire. That must have been hell.'

Remembering his own experiences in a similar position for only a week, Chavasse nodded. 'You can say that again. But why did he throw up Holy Orders? What was the given reason?'

'Difficult to discover. The Church doesn't exactly fall over itself to discuss this sort of thing. However, I've pulled a few strings and they've reluctantly given me the address of a priest who was in captivity with Rossiter. His parish is right here in London, which is rather convenient.'

Chavasse examined the card Mallory passed across. Father Henry da Souza. Portuguese, which would probably turn out to mean that his family had been living in England for at least five hundred years. 'Was there ever the slightest suggestion that Rossiter had turned Red?'

Mallory shrugged. 'Anything is possible in this worst of all possible worlds, dear boy. They certainly did a good job on him. Of course, a priest has something to hang on to; something to fight them with. Having said that, there's no question that ministers of religion held by the Chinese for a period and later released have sometimes needed psychiatric help on their return; that's how complete the brainwashing proccss has been. They've done research into it at Harvard, I understand. Anyway, you go and see Father da Souza and see what you can get out of him.'

'What about Darcy Preston?'

'No problem there, as long as he behaves himself and keeps his mouth shut. We'll put him on a plane for Jamaica tomorrow.'

'Is it all right if he stays at my place in the meantime?'

'I don't see why not.' Mallory shook his head. 'St Paul's by day and Soho by night. What a strange, mixed-up life that boy must have had.'

Chavasse got to his feet. 'He seems to have survived it all rather well. I'll be in touch later this afternoon.'

He was halfway to the door when the phone buzzed again. Mallory called him back with a gesture and picked up the receiver. He put it down again with a sigh. 'The body of a middle-aged woman wearing a lifejacket was pulled out of the sea off Weymouth by a fishing boat an hour ago. Paul, I'm sorry – damned sorry. Especially in view of what you told me.'

'So am I,' Chavasse said, and went out quietly, murder in his heart.

The Church of the Immaculate Conception was not far from the East India Docks, an area that was anything but salubrious. Chavasse parked his car on the opposite side of the road and switched off the engine. He took a cigarette from his case and offered one to Darcy Preston.

'Graham Mallory would hang, draw and quarter me if he knew I'd brought you along. On the other hand, he did tell me to keep an eye on you, and I can't very well be in two places at once.'

'You could try, but I wouldn't recommend it,' Preston said, and he got out of the car.

The church backed onto the river, a small, rather grimy pseudo-Gothic building of a kind which had been built extensively during a certain period of the nineteenth century. They went in through a porched entrance to a place of candles and shadows, incense and quiet peace. It was empty except for the man who knelt by the altar rail in a priest's cassock, white hair flaming like a halo in the candlelight.

Chavasse crossed himself and dipped a knee instinctively, although he had not practised his religion for years, and they moved down the aisle. The priest rose to his feet and was about to move towards the vestry when he saw them and paused, smiling faintly.

'Can I help you, gentlemen?'

His eyes were those of a man who loved the whole world, a rare enough breed. A bad scar ran from the right eye into the hair, but otherwise he had a face as calm and untroubled as that of a two-year-old child.

'Father da Souza? My name is Chavasse. I believe you were expecting me? This is Mr Preston, an associate.'

'Ah, yes.' Father da Souza nodded. 'Something to do with Leonard Rossiter, wasn't it?' He smiled. 'Why don't we go outside? It's rather pleasant at the moment.'

At the rear of the church, a cemetery ran down to the Thames, spiked railings fringing a low wall. There was plenty of activity on the river and the priest had been right – it was pleasant in the pale sunshine.

He sat on a tombstone and accepted a cigarette from Chavasse. 'This is nice – very nice. I often come out here to think, you know. Somehow it has the right atmosphere.' He bent his head to the match Preston held out to him and leaned back with a sigh of content. 'Now then, what was it you wanted to know about Leonard?'

'Before we go any further, Father, I think I should make it clear that this is a serious business and highly confidential. In fact, a matter of national security.'

Da Souza didn't seem perturbed in the slightest. 'Go on.'

'Would you say it was possible that Leonard Rossiter had turned Communist?'

Father da Souza examined the end of his cigarette with a slight, abstracted frown, and sighed. 'As a matter of fact, I shouldn't think there was much doubt about it.'

'I see. Have you ever spoken of this to anyone before?'

'No one ever asked me.'

Chavasse nodded. 'All right, Father, tell me all you can.'

'I was sent to work in Korea just after the Second World War. I was taken prisoner by North Korean forces a few days after the Korean War started.'

'And Rossiter?'

'Oh, I didn't meet Leonard for quite some time – nine months later, when I was moved to a special camp in Manchuria. An indoctrination centre run by the Chinese.'

'And you think Rossiter was brainwashed there?'

Father da Souza laughed gently. 'Good heavens, it isn't as easy as that, you know. They have an extraordinarily simple technique, and yet it works so very often. The original concept is Pavlovian. A question of inducing guilt or rather of magnifying the guilt that is in all of us. Shall I tell you the first thing my instructor asked me, gentlemen? Whether I had a servant at the mission to clean my room and make my bed. When I admitted that I had, he expressed surprise, produced a Bible and read me that passage in which Our Lord speaks of serving others. Yet here was I allowing one of those I had come to help to serve me. Extraordinary how guilty that one small point made me feel.'

'But your faith, Father?' Preston said. 'Wasn't it of any help at all?'

The old priest smiled beatifically. 'My son, my faith was triumphant; it overcame all odds in spite of everything that was attempted with me. I have never felt more certain of God than I did during those dark days.'

'And Rossiter?' Chavasse said. 'What about Rossiter's faith?'

The old priest looked genuinely troubled. 'I am in a difficult position here, gentlemen. I was Leonard's confessor at Nom Bek, and he mine. The secrets of the confessional are sacred. Let me say that he had problems long before he fell into Communist hands. From their point of view he was fruit that was ripe for the picking.'

'What kind of problems?'

'If I may use Marxian terminology, each man has his thesis and his antithesis. For a priest, his thesis is everything he believes in, everything he and his vocation stand for. His antithesis, on the other hand, is his darker side – the side which is present in all of us. Fears and hates, violence, aggression, the desires of the flesh. Leonard Rossiter was racked by guilt long before the instructors at Nom Bek got to work on him.'

'But why did he give up Holy Orders?'

'The official explanation was that he had experienced a crisis of faith – that he could no longer continue. This happened three or four years after his return.'

'But you think he'd fallen for the party line?'

Father da Souza nodded. 'I think it seemed to offer him what he was searching for – a strong faith – a faith which would support him.'

'You say *seemed* to offer him, Father?' Darcy Preston said.

Father da Souza smiled gently. 'One thing I can tell you with certainty. Leonard Rossiter is a soul in torment. He is like the man in Thompson's poem, pursued endlessly by the Hound of God, fleeing from the one certain hope of salvation, hell-bent on destruction because of his own self-loathing.'

Chavasse nodded slowly. 'That's all, Father. I think you've made your point.'

'I hope I've been of help. A pleasure, gentle-men.'

He shook hands and they left him there on the cracked tomb, finishing his cigarette.

'Quite a man,' Darcy Preston said as they got into the car.

'And then some.'

Mallory listened to what he had to say, a strange abstracted look on his face. 'I've spoken to NATO intelligence since you were last here.'

'About Montefiore.'

Mallory nodded. 'It's curiously disturbing, Paul. They haven't got a thing on him. Now that worries me – that really does worry me. I wouldn't mind knowing that he was the most dangerous double-agent in the game as long as one had a hint, but this whole situation smells to high heaven. How do you see it?'

Chavasse stood up and paced backwards and forwards across the room. 'Let's take the two most important strands. Colonel Ho Tsen – a very dangerous Chinese agent – and Leonard Rossiter, who seems to have fallen for the party line during his captivity. That still leaves us with the most puzzling bit of all. Why should a multi-millionaire financier like Enrico Montefiore help to further the cause of militant Chinese-style Communism? And there's another point – the immigration racket. So amateurish.'

'All right, so Rossiter's organization *is* amateurish as you say, but the Chinese don't have a great deal of choice when it comes to friends and allies. They've only got one toehold in Europe, remember – Albania. It's always possible that they just haven't realized how second-rate Rossiter's organization is.'

'You could be right,' Chavasse admitted. 'They certainly can't afford to be too choosy. Any kind of a contact in the European market is better than nothing. I suspect that might be the way they looked at it, and they can be naïve. People are always telling us that we don't understand the Orientals. That may be true, but they certainly don't understand us any better.'

Mallory sat there staring into space for perhaps thirty seconds, then he nodded. 'Right,

Paul, it's all yours. Find them – all three of them. Ho Tsen, Rossiter and Montefiore. I'd like to know what it's all about, but the most important thing is to bring them to a stop.'

'A dead stop?'

'Naturally. Seek and destroy. I can't see any point in taking half-measures. It's completely your baby from now on. Use the usual communication system whenever possible to keep me informed. See Jean on your way out about money. Anything else?'

Chavasse nodded. 'The man you've got keeping an eye on this bloke Gorman at Fixby – pull him off.'

'You're going down there yourself?'

'It would seem as good a place as any to start.'

Mallory reached for the phone. 'I'll see to it now. Good luck.'

Jean Frazer glanced up as Chavasse emerged. 'You look pleased with yourself.'

'I am.'

Chavasse helped himself to a cigarette from the box on her desk. His eyes were like black glass in the dark Celtic face. He looked like the devil himself, and for some reason she shivered.

'What is it, Paul?'

'I'm not too sure,' he said. 'It's been a long time since I felt like this.'

'Like what?'

'Personally involved in something. Me, Paul Chavasse, not just the Bureau. I'm thinking of an old man on his back on a south-coast beach this morning who only wanted to see his son, and a fussy little woman who died alone, utterly terrified. A silly, stupid little woman who never hurt anyone in her life.'

He sighed heavily and stubbed out his cigarette. 'I want revenge, Jean. For the first time, I want to take care of someone permanently for personal reasons. It's a new sensation. What worries me is how happy I feel about the prospect.'

He parted from Darcy Preston with regret, for he had come to like the brilliant, sardonic Jamaican – and not only because of what they had been through together. As he packed one or two things, Darcy sat on the window seat and watched. He was wearing a pair of Chavasse's trousers, a polo-neck sweater and a sports jacket in Donegal tweed.

'Sure you're okay for cash?' Chavasse asked as he locked his suitcase.

Darcy nodded. 'I still have a bank account here.'

Chavasse buttoned an old naval bridge coat that gave him rather a nautical air. 'I don't suppose I'll be seeing you again. By this time tomorrow, you'll be on your way to sunny Jamaica.'

'Land of carefree calypso and shanty towns. Give me Birmingham any day.' Darcy grinned. 'And what about you? Where do you start? At this place, Fixby?'

'Good a place as any.'

The Jamaican held out his hand. 'This is it, then. Good luck, Paul, and next time you see Rossiter, give him one for me. Preferably with your boot.'

Chavasse had the door half-open when Darcy spoke again. 'Just one thing. It's been eating away at me, so I've got to ask. Why did they kill Harvey that way?'

'I can only guess. They were probably in danger of being boarded. In a manner of speaking, they were destroying the evidence.'

Darcy Preston actually laughed. 'You know something, that's really ironic. That's exactly what the blackbirders did with their slaves in the old days when the Royal Navy was on their tail – put them over the side in chains.'

He laughed again, but this time there were tears in his eyes and Chavasse closed the door and left him there, alone with his grief in the quiet room.

# 10

Fixby was a village in decline, the sort of place that had enjoyed a mild prosperity when fishing was still an economic proposition, but not now. The young ones had left for the big city and most of the cottages had been taken over by town-dwellers seeking a weekend refuge.

Chavasse had himself driven to Weymouth in a Bureau car and completed his journey on the local bus. It was four o'clock in the afternoon when it deposited him in Fixby, where he was the only passenger to alight.

The single street was deserted and the pub, in strict adherence with the English licensing laws, had its door firmly shut. He moved past it and continued towards the creek, one hand pushed in the pocket of his old bridge coat, a slim leather locked briefcase swinging from the other.

The boatyard wasn't hard to find, a ghost of a place, a graveyard of hopes and ships, beached like dead whales, sombre in the rain. There was an office of sorts, a decaying clapboard house behind. There didn't seem to be anyone about and he moved towards the jetty.

A sea-going launch was moored there, a trim craft if ever he'd seen one. She was rigged for big-game fishing, with a couple of swivel chairs fitted to the stern deck and a steel hoist.

She was a beautiful boat, there was no doubt about that – a jewel in a jungle of weeds. He stood there looking at her for quite a while, then turned away.

A man was standing watching him from the shadow of an old barge. He was very tall and thin and dressed in an old reefer jacket, peaked cap and greasy overalls. His face was his most remarkable feature. It was the face of a Judas, one eye turned into the corner, the mouth like a knife-slash, a face as repulsively fascinating as a medieval gargoyle.

'Admiring her, are you?' His voice was hardly more than a whisper, and as he approached

Chavasse noticed a jagged scar that stretched from his right ear to his windpipe.

'She's quite a boat.'

'She certainly is. Penta engines, radar, echo-sounder. All that and thirty-five knots. You know boats?'

'A little. Are you Gorman?'

'That's right. What can I do for you?'

'I'd like to take a little trip if your boat is available.'

'Fishing?' Gorman shook his head. 'Too late in the day.'

'I was thinking of rather more than that,' Chavasse said. 'The fact is I want to get across the Channel in a hurry, and a friend of mine told me you might be able to oblige at a price.'

Gorman looked down the creek, whistling softly. 'Who is this friend?' he asked, after a short pause.

Chavasse managed to look suitably embarrassed. 'To tell you the truth, he wasn't really a friend. Just a bloke I met in a bar in Soho. He said that any time I wanted to get out of the country in a hurry, you were a good man to see.'

Gorman turned abruptly and spoke over his shoulder as he walked away. 'Come up to the office. It's going to rain.'

Chavasse went after him and mounted the rickety wooden stairs to the verandah. At the top he paused and turned his head sharply, aware of some kind of movement down there among the derelict boats. A dog, perhaps, or a rabbit. But it left him with a vague unease as he went into the office.

The place was cluttered with odds and ends of every description. Gorman cleared the table with a sweep of an arm and produced a bottle of whisky and two glasses.

'So you want to get across the water pretty badly?' he said.

Chavasse placed his case on the table and unlocked it. He lifted a shirt and uncovered a thousand pounds made up of several neat bundles of English fivers and French francs. It looked considerably more than it was, and Gorman's bad eye rolled wildly.

Chavasse took out two bundles of fivers and pushed them across. 'That's how badly I want to get across, Gorman. Is it a deal?'

Gorman's smile was so evil as to be almost seraphic. He scooped up the cash and stowed it away in a battered wallet. 'When do you want to leave?'

'The sooner the better, as far as I'm concerned.'

Gorman smiled again, that same seraphic smile. 'Then what are we waiting for?' he demanded, and led the way out.

The boat was called the *Mary Grant* and she was every bit as good as she looked. Chavasse stood at the rail as they moved down the creek towards the open sea and took a few deep breaths of the salt air. It was good to be on the move again, even towards an unknown future. In fact, if he was honest with himself, that accounted for a great deal of the fascination in his work – quite simply the living from day to day, not knowing what lay around the next corner.

Waves started to slap against the hull with strange little hollow sounds that vibrated through the whole boat as they left the shelter of the

creek and lifted to meet the Channel swell.
He moved to the wheelhouse and paused in
the doorway.

'Where were you thinking of putting me
down?'

'Anywhere you like,' Gorman said. 'You're
the boss.'

'I was thinking of somewhere a little bit off the
beaten track. The Golfe de St-Malo or Brittany.
I could move on to Marseille from there.'

'Suits me.'

Gorman altered course a couple of points
and Chavasse said, 'I'll go below and try to
get some sleep.'

'Best thing to do. Could get a little rough in
mid-Channel. The glass is falling. You'll find
coffee in the big Thermos in the galley.'

Chavasse went below to the main saloon. He
was tired – damned tired – which was hardly
surprising. He found the coffee in the galley,
poured himself a cup and returned to the saloon.
He drank slowly, going over the situation point
by point. There was nothing to be gained from a
confrontation with Gorman just yet; that could
come later.

Quite suddenly, his brain almost ceased to function. God, but he was tired. He stretched out on the padded seat and stared up at the bulkhead. The ribs in the roof seemed to undulate slowly, like ripples on the surface of a pond, and his mouth was strangely dry. It was only in the final moment of his plunge into darkness that it occurred to his bemused brain that something might have gone wrong.

He surfaced slowly, for the first few moments, aware only of existing. The saloon was in darkness, that much was obvious, and he was lying face-down on the padded seat. He tried to move, lost his balance and fell to the floor, which was hardly surprising considering that his wrists were securely lashed behind his back.

The *Mary Grant* was still moving, but as he tried to scramble to his feet, the engines were cut and she started to drift. There was a footstep on the companionway, the light was switched on, and Gorman appeared. He squatted so close that Chavasse was aware of the stale smell of sweat from his unwashed body.

'How are you then, matey?' Gorman patted his cheek.

'What's the game?' Chavasse demanded, staying with his role for the time being. 'I thought we had a deal.'

Gorman got up and opened the slim case, which stood on the table. He took out one of the packets of banknotes. 'This is the game, matey – the green stuff. I've always had a fellow-feeling for it. It makes me come out in goose-pimples all over. This little collection, I like so much that I can't bear to be separated from any part of it.'

'Okay,' Chavasse said. 'I won't give you any trouble. Just drop me off at the other end, that's all I ask.'

Gorman's laugh was something to be heard as he pulled him to his feet and pushed him towards the companionway. 'I'll drop you off all right, matey, make no mistake about that. Right into the deep end.'

It was cold on deck, rain drifting down through the yellow light. Chavasse turned to face him. Gorman picked up a length of rusty anchor chain, and Chavasse said calmly, 'Who taught you that little trick – Rossiter?'

It certainly brought Gorman to a stop. He glared at Chavasse, his eye rolling horribly, and when he spoke his voice was the merest whisper.

'Who are you? What is this?'

'It's no good, Gorman,' Chavasse told him flatly. 'My people know where I am. When I end up missing, you'll have some tall explaining to do.'

He had completely miscalculated his man. Gorman gave a cry of rage, and his arm went back to strike, the length of chain cracking out like a leather whip

It never landed. A hand emerged from the shadows and wrenched the chain from his grasp. Gorman spun round and Darcy Preston stepped into the light.

Gorman didn't mess about. His hand went into his pocket and came out clutching a revolver, but he made the mistake of firing too quickly. The bullet ploughed into the deckhouse and Darcy went headfirst into the sea.

Gorman peered into the dark waters and, behind him, Preston pulled himself over the rail, having swum under the keel. There was only one possible weapon, a long-handled gaff used for pulling in game fish, which hung on the side of the wheelhouse in a spring clip. As he pulled it free, the clip twanged musically and Gorman turned.

This time he went by the manual. His arm swung up in a straight line as he sighted along the barrel with his good eye. Chavasse went for him, shoulder down like a rugby forward, sending him staggering against the rail. The revolver discharged harmlessly, and as Gorman straightened, aiming again, Darcy lunged with the gaff, the point catching Gorman in the right armpit. He went over the rail backwards with a cry. By the time Chavasse got there, the dark waters had closed over his head.

'Hold out your hands,' Darcy ordered, and sliced through Chavasse's bonds with the edge of the razor-sharp gaff.

Chavasse turned, massaging his wrists to restore the circulation. 'Now that's what I call a timely intervention. Is it permissible to enquire where in the hell you sprang from?'

'Glad to oblige,' Darcy said. 'After you'd left, I thought about things for at least five minutes, then went downstairs to the garage and helped myself to your car. I left it at Hurn Airport and came the rest of the way by taxi. I was actually in Fixby before you.'

'Then what?'

'Oh, I hung around the boatyard awaiting events, as they say. I heard most of your conversation with Gorman, waited till you'd gone into the office, then came on board and hid in the chain locker.'

'You certainly took your own sweet time about showing up, or was that just your sense of the dramatic?'

'As a matter of fact, I fell asleep. Didn't wake up till Gorman started thumping around and making all that noise.'

Chavasse sighed. 'All right, what are you doing here?'

'It's quite simple. My brother was a criminal by every possible standard. He was a thief and a gangster, but he was good to me. If I said that I loved such a man, could you accept that?'

'Perfectly,' Chavasse told him gravely.

'He didn't deserve to die that way, Paul.

163

He deserved many things in this life, but not that. When the time comes, I am going to kill Leonard Rossiter personally. We Jamaicans are a religious people, a proud people. An eye for an eye, the Book says, no more, no less. I will have Rossiter's life then, for that is the just thing.'

Chavasse nodded soberly. 'I respect your feelings, I understand them, but between the thought and the deed is often a very wide gap, especially for a man like you. I can kill when I have to, quickly, expertly and without a second thought, because I'm a professional. Can you be that certain?'

'We'll have to see, won't we?'

'Fair enough. I'll get this thing moving, you dry yourself. We'll talk things over later.'

The Jamaican nodded and disappeared into the companionway. Chavasse went along the deck to the wheelhouse and started the engines. They made a fine satisfying growl and he pushed up the throttle and took the *Mary Grant* into the night with a burst of power.

\*      \*      \*

'I always wanted to be a boxer,' Darcy said.

He leaned against the closed door of the wheelhouse, a blanket around his shoulders, a mug of tea in one hand, almost invisible in the darkness.

'What did Harvey have to say to that?'

Darcy chuckled. 'He argued in percentages and he certainly saw no percentage in that. He always said a good fighter was a hungry fighter and I was anything but hungry. Mind you, he indulged me up to a certain point. I had lessons from some of the best pro fighters in the game. He had an interest in a gym in Whitechapel.'

'What made you choose the law?'

'With my background? A hell of a lot of people found that one funny. On the other hand, I knew every crook in Soho, which came in useful when I started to practise.'

'You were constantly in demand?'

'Something like that. I cleared out after Harvey's trial because I realized I simply couldn't continue with the kind of double life I had been leading. Went out to Jamaica and started again. A good move. That's where I met my wife.'

'Time and chance,' Chavasse said.

'As I told your Mr Mallory, Harvey got a letter to me detailing what he intended to do. When he didn't turn up, friends notified me and I decided to follow in his footsteps. It seemed the logical thing.'

'Does your wife know?'

Darcy grinned. 'She thinks I'm in New York on legal business.' He emptied his mug and put it on the chart table. 'And what about you? How did you get into this kind of work?'

'Time and chance again.' Chavasse shrugged. 'I have a language kink. Soak them up like water into a sponge – no work in it at all. I was lecturing in a provincial university and finding it pretty boring, when a friend asked me to help him get his sister out of Czechoslovakia. It had a ring of adventure to it, so I gave it a go.'

'And succeeded?'

'Only just. I was in an Austrian hospital with a bullet in my leg when Mallory came to see me and offered me a job. That was twelve years ago.'

'Any regrets?'

'It's too late for regrets. Far too late. Now

let's come back to the present and discuss what we're going to do when we arrive at Ste-Denise.'

# BRITTANY

# 11

They made such excellent time that it was only nine-thirty in the evening as they approached Ste-Denise. There was a small bay with a deep-water channel marked on the chart about a quarter of a mile to the east, and Chavasse decided to give it a try.

He couldn't have made a better choice. The bay was almost a complete circle, no more than a hundred yards in diameter and guarded by high cliffs which gave excellent cover from the sea. They dropped anchor and went below.

Chavasse put his leather business case on the table, opened it and tossed a couple of packets of francs across to Darcy. 'Half for you, half for me. Just in case.'

'You mean I'm getting paid, too?'

Darcy stowed the money away in an inside

pocket and Chavasse pressed a hidden catch and removed the false bottom of the case to reveal an interior compartment. Expertly packed away inside were a Smith & Wesson .38 Magnum revolver, a Walther PPK and a machine pistol.

Darcy whistled softly. 'What is this, Prohibition?'

'Nothing like being prepared.' Chavasse offered him the Smith & Wesson. 'Guaranteed not to jam. About the best man-stopper I know.' He dropped the Walther into his pocket, and replaced the false bottom in the case and stowed it away in a locker under the table. 'And now for the most interesting act of the evening.'

They rowed ashore in the fibreglass dinghy, beached it and scaled the cliffs by means of a narrow path. The sky was blue-black, and every star gleamed like white fire. There was no moon, yet a strange luminosity hung over everything, giving them a range of vision much greater than might have reasonably been expected under the circumstances. They made rapid progress through the scattered pines and soon came to a point from which they could look down into Ste-Denise.

There was a light here and there in the cottages and several in the downstairs windows of the Running Man.

'How do you intend to play this thing?' Darcy asked.

'By ear,' Chavasse told him. 'Strictly by ear. Let's see how many guests are at the party first.'

They went down the hill, scrambled across a fence and continued along a narrow country lane that soon brought them to the outskirts of the village. Here, the cottages were spaced well apart, each with its own small patch of ground under cultivation.

They passed the first house, and as they approached the second, Darcy placed a hand on Chavasse's sleeve. 'This is Mercier's place, or did you know?'

'Now that is interesting,' Chavasse said softly. 'Let's take a look.'

They moved across the cobbled yard and crouched by the window. Light reached out with gold fingers into the darkness, and through a gap in the curtain they could see Mercier sitting at the kitchen table, head bowed, a bottle of brandy and a tin mug in front of him.

173

'He doesn't look too happy,' Darcy breathed.

Chavasse nodded. 'Didn't you say something about his wife being an invalid?'

'That's right. Hasn't been out of bed in four years.'

'Then she's hardly likely to interfere if we're quiet. Knock on the door and then get out of sight. I'll handle him.'

Mercier was slow in responding and his footsteps dragged strangely across the stone floor. He opened the door and peered out, took a step forward, an anxious, expectant look on his face. Chavasse touched the barrel of the gun to his temple.

'One cry and you're a dead man, Mercier. Inside.'

Mercier moved backwards and Chavasse went after him, Preston close behind. He closed the door and Mercier looked from one to the other then laughed abruptly.

'This'll be a surprise for Jacaud. He told me you were both dead.'

'Where is he?'

'At the Running Man, entertaining his cronies from the village.'

'And Rossiter?'

Mercier shrugged. 'They came back this morning, just before noon, in the Englishman's boat.'

'That would be a man called Gorman?'

Mercier nodded. 'We've done a lot of business with him in the past. He's always in and out of here.'

'What about the authorities?'

'In these parts, monsieur?' Mercier shrugged. 'People mind their own business.'

Chavasse nodded. 'What happened to Rossiter and the others? Are they still at the Running Man?'

Mercier shook his head. 'Monsieur Rossiter left just after noon in the Renault. He took the Indian girl and the Chinese man with him. The Chinese was heavily bandaged about the face.'

'How did the girl look?'

'How would you expect her to look, monsieur? As beautiful as ever.'

'I don't mean that. Did she seem afraid at all – afraid of Rossiter?'

Mercier shook his head. 'On the contrary, monsieur. She looked at him as if he were . . .'

He seemed to have difficulty in finding the right word. 'As if he were . . .'

'God?' Darcy Preston suggested.

'Something like that, monsieur.'

He was strangely calm and unafraid and the answers came so readily. Chavasse let it go for the moment and carried on. 'Where did they go?'

'I haven't the slightest idea.'

'Come off it, Mercier, you can do better than that. Try Hellgate for a start, and Montefiore – don't tell me you've never heard of them?'

'Of course, monsieur. I have heard those two names on several occasions – snatches of conversation between Jacaud and Monsieur Rossiter, but that is all. To me they are names and nothing more.'

He was speaking the truth, Chavasse was certain, which didn't seem to make any kind of sense.

'What's happened, Mercier?' he said softly. 'You're a different man.'

Mercier turned without a word, walked to a door, opened it and stood to one side. 'Messieurs,' he said, with a small hopeless gesture.

Chavasse and Preston moved to join him and looked into a small, cluttered sitting room. A plain wooden coffin rested on the table, a candle at each end.

Chavasse closed the door gently. 'Your wife?'

Mercier nodded. 'Not a day without pain for four years, monsieur, and yet she never complained, although she knew there could be only one end. I tried everything. Big doctors from Brest, expensive medicines – all for nothing.'

'That must have cost money?'

Mercier nodded. 'How else do you think I came to be working for an animal like Jacaud? For my Nanette – only for Nanette. It was for her that I endured so much horror. For her and her alone that I kept my mouth shut.'

'You're saying you went in fear of your life?'

Mercier shook his head. 'No, monsieur, in fear for my wife's life; of what that devil Rossiter might do to her.'

'He made such threats?'

'To keep me quiet. He had to, monsieur, particularly after a trip some weeks ago when I sailed on the *Leopard* as deckhand.'

'What happened then?'

177

Mercier hesitated, and Chavasse said, 'Let me tell you what happened after we left here last night. The *Leopard* went down in the Channel, did Jacaud tell you that?'

'He said there had been an accident. That the engine had exploded and that the rest of you had been killed.'

'He and Rossiter left us to drown, locked in the saloon,' Chavasse said. 'The woman and the old man died trying to swim ashore.'

Mercier looked genuinely shocked. 'My God, they are animals, not men. Why, only the other week, monsieur, on the occasion I was speaking of earlier, we were sighted off the English coast by a British torpedo-boat. We had only one passenger at the time – a special trip for some reason.' He turned to Darcy. 'A West Indian like you, monsieur.'

Preston's face had tightened and he looked ill. 'What happened?'

'Rossiter said we'd get seven years if we were caught with him aboard. He put him over the side, wrapped in chains – and he was still alive. Still alive. Sometimes in my dreams I can still see the look in his eyes when Rossiter put him over the rail.'

Darcy nodded blindly. 'And he told you he'd kill your wife if you didn't keep quiet.'

'That's right, monsieur.'

Darcy turned abruptly, wrenched open the door and went out. Mercier looked bewildered and Chavasse said quietly, 'His brother – his brother, Mercier. We've come to settle the account. Will you help us?'

Mercier took a reefer jacket from behind the door and pulled it on. 'Anything, monsieur.'

'Good. This is what you will do. Wait by the Running Man and watch the harbour. In a little while, you will see the *Mary Grant* come in. You know her?'

'Of course, monsieur, Gorman's boat.'

'You will enter The Running Man and tell Jacaud that Gorman has returned and is waiting urgently for him down at the jetty. Make sure that other people hear you tell him this.'

'And afterwards?'

'Do you have a boat of your own?'

Mercier nodded. 'An old whaleboat with a diesel engine.'

'Good – when we leave the harbour we will go to a bay called Panmarch. You know it?'

179

'As I know every inch of this coast.'

'We'll wait for you there.' Chavasse slapped him on the shoulder. 'We will fix him, our brave Jacaud, eh, Mercier?'

Mercier's eyes glowed with fire, the hatred of years boiling over, and they went out together.


There were perhaps a dozen fishermen in the bar when Mercier entered the Running Man, and Jacaud was holding court. They pressed round eagerly as he poured red wine from an earthenware jug, leaving a trail like blood across the counter while the old woman who worked for him looked on with a tight mouth.

'Free,' he roared. 'Everything on me. In the morning, I'll be away and you'll never see old Jacaud again.'

Mercier had difficulty forcing his way through to the bar, but when Jacaud noticed him, he greeted him effusively.

'Mercier, old friend, where have you been hiding?'

His speech was slurred and he gave every appearance of being drunk. Mercier was instantly suspicious, never having seen him the worse for liquor in his whole life.

'I've got a message for you,' he said loudly. 'From Monsieur Gorman.'

Several heads turned in interest and Jacaud frowned, instantly sober. 'Gorman? He is here?'

'At the jetty. He just came in on the *Mary Grant*.'

Jacaud put down the jug and nodded to the old woman. 'It's all yours.' He came round the bar and brushed past Mercier. 'Let's go.'

Outside, a slight wind moved in from the sea and stirred the pines. 'Did he say what he wanted? Is it trouble?'

Mercier shrugged. 'Why should he talk to me, Monsieur Jacaud, a person of no importance? He told me nothing.'

Jacaud glared at him in surprise, aware of a new belligerency in his tone, but there was no time to investigate now. At the end of the street, Mercier paused.

'I leave you here, monsieur.'

'You are going home?'

'That's right.'

Jacaud tried to inject a little friendliness into

181

his voice. 'I'll drop in later, if I may, after I've
seen what Gorman wants. I'd like to talk things
over with you now that I'm leaving.'

'As you wish, monsieur.'

Mercier faded into the night and Jacaud continued on his way, walking quickly, without
even the slightest hint of drunkenness in his
manner. If anything, he was worried, for he was
not over-endowed with intelligence. Rossiter
had left him strict instructions as to what he
was to do and Gorman hadn't entered into
them at all.

The *Mary Grant* waited at the jetty, her
engines whispering quietly. He went down the
ladder to the deck and paused uncertainly. There
was a movement in the wheelhouse and he went
towards it quickly.

'Gorman?' he demanded hoarsely.

He reached the door, and the heart in him
seemed to stop beating, for the face that stared
coldly at him from the darkness, disembodied in the light from the binnacle, was one
which he had never expected to see again in
this life.

Chavasse smiled gently. 'Come right in, Jacaud.'

Jacaud took a step back and the muzzle of a revolver touched him on the temple. He turned his head involuntarily and found himself looking straight at Darcy Preston.

Sweat sprang to his forehead, cold as death, and he started to shake, for what he was seeing simply could not be. He sagged against the wheelhouse door with a groan, and the *Mary Grant* left the jetty and moved out to sea.

By the time they had anchored in Panmarch Bay, Jacaud no longer believed in ghosts, only in miracles, and a miracle was something which could happen to anyone. His awe had been replaced by anger and he awaited his chance to strike. It came when Mercier arrived and tied up alongside in his old whaleboat. Preston went to catch the line he threw, leaving Chavasse in charge, who suddenly seemed to get careless. Jacaud grabbed for the gun he was holding; Chavasse, who had been anticipating just such a move, swayed to one side and clouted him over the head.

The blow would have dazed any other man, sending him to his knees for several minutes. Jacaud simply rolled on one shoulder, came to his feet and dived for the rail. Darcy managed to get a foot under him just in time and Jacaud went sprawling.

When he got to his feet, he found Preston taking off his jacket. 'Come on then, Jacaud,' he said. 'Let's see how good you are.'

'You black ape.'

Jacaud came in like a tornado, great arms flailing, hands reaching out to destroy, and proceeded to get the thrashing of his life as Darcy demolished him with a scientific exactitude that was awe-inspiring in its economy. The Jamaican in action was something to see, and hatred gave him an additional advantage.

Jacaud landed perhaps three or four punches, but everything else he threw only touched air. In return, he was subjected to a barrage of punches that were devastating in their effect, driving him to his knees again and again until a final right cross put him on his back.

He lay there sobbing for breath, and Darcy dropped to one knee beside him. 'And now,

Jacaud, you will answer some questions, quickly and accurately.'

Jacaud spat in his face.

Chavasse pulled Darcy up. 'Take a breather. Let me try.' He lit a cigarette. 'We all hate you here, Jacaud. The Jamaican, because you and Rossiter drowned his brother. Mercier, because you dragged him down into the filth with you. Me, because I don't like your smell. You're an animal – something from under a stone – and I'd no more hesitate to kill you than I would to step on a slug. Now that we know where we stand, we'll try again. Where has Rossiter gone?'

Jacaud's reply was coarse and to the point.

Chavasse stood up. 'On your feet.'

Jacaud hesitated and Mercier kicked him in the ribs. 'You heard the gentleman.'

Jacaud got up reluctantly and Chavasse tossed Darcy a coil of rope. 'Tie his wrists.'

Jacaud didn't bother to struggle. 'You can do what you like, you won't make me talk. I'll see you in hell first.'

He raved on for some time, but Chavasse ignored him and walked to the stern, where the swivel seats were fastened to the deck for big-game fishing and the hoist and pulley were rigged ready to haul in tuna or shark.

'Let's have him down here.'

Darcy pushed Jacaud forward, and Chavasse swung him around and looped his bonds over the hook on the end of the pulley line. 'Here, what is this?' Jacaud demanded.

Chavasse nodded to the other two. 'Haul away.'

As Preston and Mercier turned the winch handle between them, Jacaud's feet left the deck, and in a moment he was three feet up in the air. He started to struggle, kicking wildly, and Chavasse pushed the hoist out over the water. Jacaud hung there, cursing, and Chavasse tried again.

'Ready to talk, Jacaud?'

'To hell with you – to hell with all of you.'

Chavasse nodded, Darcy released the winch handle and Jacaud disappeared beneath the surface. Chavasse gave him a full minute, checking his watch carefully, then nodded and Darcy and Mercier cranked him in.

Jacaud hung just beyond the rail, chest heaving as he sobbed for breath. He started to

186

cough, then vomited. Chavasse gave him a moment to collect himself.

'Hellgate, Jacaud, and Montefiore. I want to know about both of them.'

Jacaud cursed him, kicking out wildly. Chavasse turned and nodded, his face cold, and the winch creaked again.

This time he made it one minute and a half, and when Jacaud appeared there was hardly any movement at all. Chavasse swung him in, and after a while the great head lifted and the eyes opened.

'Hellgate,' he croaked. 'It's a house in the Camargue near a village called Chatillon. Monsieur Montefiore owns it.'

'And that's where Rossiter and the others have gone?' Jacaud nodded weakly. 'And Montefiore, is he there now?'

'I don't know. I've never met him. I only know what Rossiter has told me.'

'Why didn't you leave with the others?'

'Rossiter wanted me to take care of Mercier – he thought he knew too much and he wanted me to leave openly so that questions would not be asked. I only had a lease on the inn. It's up

JACK HIGGINS

in a couple of months anyway, so I made it over to the old hag who works for me. I told everyone I was leaving for Corsica tomorrow. That I'd been left a farm by a distant relative.'

Chavasse nodded slowly. 'So, you were to kill Mercier?'

Jacaud started to cough, then gave a strange choking cry. His body heaved as if he was in pain and Mercier and Darcy lowered him to the deck quickly. Mercier dropped to his knees and put an ear against Jacaud's chest. When he looked up, his face was grave.

'He is dead, monsieur. His heart has given out.'

'Let's hope he told the truth then,' Chavasse said calmly. 'Get the ropes off him and put him in the saloon.'

He turned and Darcy grabbed him by the arm. 'Is that all you can say, for God's sake? We've just killed a man.'

'One way or the other, he was due for it,' Chavasse said. 'So cut out the hearts and flowers. I haven't got time.'

He pulled free and went into the wheelhouse. He was examining the chart when they joined

188

him. 'I need a nice deep channel,' he said to Mercier. 'Deep enough for the *Mary Grant* to sink into without trace.'

Mercier sighed. 'A pity, monsieur. It's a beautiful boat.'

'She's still got to go,' Chavasse said. 'Where would you suggest?'

Mercier considered the chart for a moment or two, then jabbed a finger at a group of rocks marked as dangerous about six miles out.

'The Pinnacles, monsieur, they've taken plenty of ships in their time. They stick up from a trench a thousand feet deep. Anything that goes down there will stay down, believe me.'

Chavasse nodded. 'That's it, then. You lead the way in the whaler. I'll follow. Go with him, Darcy.'

'I'll stay with you.'

Chavasse shook his head. 'No point, this kind of job only needs one.'

'I said I'd stay.' Darcy's voice was bleak. 'What I say, I mean.'

He moved into the prow and stood there with his hands in his pockets, shoulders hunched.

189

'I don't think he is too happy, monsieur,' Mercier commented. 'Which surprises me. After all, they did as much to his own brother.'

'Which is exactly what's bothering him,' Chavasse said. 'He isn't a hunting animal, Mercier. Now let's get moving. We haven't much time.'

The Pinnacles were first observed as patches of white water in the distance. As the boats approached, the turbulence increased and Chavasse was aware of great plumes of spray that blossomed in the night.

The Pinnacles themselves were a scattered group of jagged rocks, in some cases permanently awash, and in others, twenty or thirty feet above the waves. When Mercier whistled sharply and waved, the agreed signal, Chavasse cut the engines and called to Darcy, who had been waiting by the forward hatch with a fire axe. Now he dropped inside and began to batter a series of holes in the prow. When he reappeared, she was already settling at that end and he was soaked to the skin.

Chavasse unfastened a cork lifebelt bearing the ship's name and tossed it overboard as Mercier came alongside.

'Lost at sea,' he said. 'Sunk with all hands. Nobody will ever see Jacaud again.'

'And Gorman?' Darcy asked. 'What about him?'

Chavasse shrugged. 'Believe it or not, but most people who take a dive into the Channel don't turn up again. Even if somebody does find what's left of him after a few weeks, it'll all fit neatly.'

'You have a naturally tidy mind,' Darcy said.

'Too complicated. I'm a professional, you're not. It's as simple as that.'

The whaleboat closed in and they scrambled aboard. Mercier took her round in a wide circle and they watched. The *Mary Grant* was well down by the head now, her stern lifting out of the water. When she went, she disappeared so quickly that if any one of them had closed his eyes momentarily, he would have missed it. The waters rolled over and Mercier opened the throttle and took the whaler away.

'And now what?' Darcy Preston demanded,

191

dropping down on one of the wide seats, shoulders hunched against the spray.

'We catch a train,' Chavasse said. 'A train for Marseille, if there is one, or is it still we?'

Darcy nodded slowly. 'I've gone too far now to step back. You needn't worry – I'll be behind you all the way.'

'Fair enough.' Chavasse turned to Mercier. 'Take us to some quiet spot on the coast as near to St-Brieuc as possible. Can you manage that?'

'Certainly, monsieur.'

Chavasse gave him a cigarette and held out a match in cupped hands. 'About Jacaud, Mercier, there could be questions.'

'Perhaps, monsieur, but I doubt it. He was to leave in the morning. Most people will think he left a little earlier. In any case, he was seen to go out in the *Mary Grant*, and where is the *Mary Grant* now? Perhaps in a few days that lifebelt will be found by a fishing boat or drift ashore somewhere, and perhaps not. Henri Jacaud never existed, monsieur.'

'And you? What will you do?'

'I will bury my wife,' Mercier said simply.

# FRANCE
## THE CAMARGUE

# 12

It was just before midnight when they reached St-Brieuc. By chance there was a train due out in fifteen minutes to Rennes, and Chavasse decided to take it rather than hang about.

At Rennes they had a delay of an hour and a half before the Marseille train and spent it in a café just outside the station. The Jamaican was still brooding and had little to say for himself. In the end, Chavasse had had enough.

'It's no good going on like this,' he said. 'Either we clear the air now or you drop out.'

'Wouldn't that be something of a problem?' Darcy said. 'I'm not even in this country officially.'

Chavasse shook his head. 'I can contact our Paris office. They'll get you out.'

Darcy looked genuinely troubled. 'I don't

know, Paul. When I first got the idea of following you, it seemed to make sense, and especially later when I heard what they'd done to Harvey. I was bitter and angry, I wanted revenge.'

'So?'

'That business with Gorman, I didn't mind that. After all, he was trying to kill you. There was nothing else I could do. But Jacaud.' He shook his head. 'That sticks in my throat.'

'If that's the way you feel, then you'd better leave,' Chavasse told him. 'Rossiter drowned your brother like a rat and without a qualm, he tried his hand at mass murder when the *Leopard* went down and didn't do so badly when you remember what happened to Mrs Campbell and old Hamid. He won't hesitate to see the both of us off the moment he claps eyes on us and realizes we're still in the land of the living. This isn't the Old Bailey or the Jamaican High Court. There's only one law here – kill or be killed – and I've had direct orders. Ho Tsen, Rossiter and Montefiore – they've all got to go.'

The Jamaican shook his head. 'You know, back there in the old days, living with Harvey in Soho, I met every kind of villain there was, but you – you're in a class of your own.'

'Which is why I've survived twelve years at this bloody game,' Chavasse said. 'Now are you in or out?'

'The way I see it, I don't really have much choice in the matter. I know that once I get anywhere near Rossiter, if I don't get him first, he'll get me. It goes against the grain, that's all, to accept that that's the way it is. I had years of it in Harvey's particular jungle – I don't suppose a psychologist would have much difficulty in working out why I took to the law.' He sighed heavily. 'But you can count on me, Paul. I won't let you down.'

'Good, now I know where I am I'll put a call through to our field agent in Marseille. I'd like him to be ready for us when we arrive in the morning.'

He stood up and Darcy said, 'This place, the Camargue – what is it exactly?'

'The delta area at the mouth of the Rhône,' Chavasse told him. 'About three hundred square miles of lagoons and waterways, marshes, white sand dunes and hot sun, though this isn't the best time of the year for that. It's famous for three things. White horses, fighting bulls and flamingoes. I was there as a boy twenty years ago and I've never forgotten it.'

'But what in the hell are they doing in a place like that?' Darcy demanded.

'That remains to be seen, doesn't it?' Chavasse said and went to make his phone call.

Jacob Malik was Polish by birth and had left the country of his origin for political reasons just before the outbreak of the Second World War. For a couple of years, he had worked for the Deuxième Bureau, the old French secret service organization which had died in 1940. He had spent the war working with the British Special Operations Executive, acting as a courier to French Resistance units. An adventurous career had been brought to an end by an FLN grenade through his hotel bedroom window during the Algerian troubles. He had retired to a small café on the Marseille waterfront with his Moorish wife and three children. He had been acting as Bureau agent in that city for six years and Chavasse had worked with him twice.

He was standing beside a Renault estate-car leaning heavily on his walking stick when they emerged from the station, a thin, elegant-looking man with a spiked moustache who carried his sixty years well.

He limped towards them and greeted Chavasse with enthusiasm. 'My dear Paul, how wonderful to see you. How goes it?'

'Excellent.' Chavasse took his hand warmly. 'And Nerida and your family?'

'Blooming. She still misses Algiers, but we could never go back. I wouldn't last a week. They have long memories, those people.'

Chavasse introduced him to Darcy and they all got into the Renault and drove away. It was warm and rather sultry, the sun hidden from view by heavy grey clouds, and yet there was that intense light common to Marseille, dazzling to the eyes.

'What have you arranged?' Chavasse asked.

'I gave the whole thing a great deal of thought after your phone call,' Malik said. 'At exactly four a.m. I hit upon an idea of some genius, though I say this with all due modesty. To get into the Camargue presents no problem. To stay without being observed is impossible.'

'In three hundred square miles of lagoon and marsh?' Chavasse said. 'I don't follow.'

'Oh, the population is small enough, mainly wildflowers and a few cowboys who tend the young bulls and the horses which run wild in all parts of the area. It is because of the sparseness of the population that it is difficult for outsiders to enter without it being known. What you need is a legitimate reason for being there, a reason which anyone who sees you will accept.'

'And you've found it?'

'Birdwatching,' Malik said simply.

Darcy Preston laughed out loud. 'He can't be serious.'

'But I am.' Malik looked slightly injured. 'The Camargue is famous for its wild birds, particularly its colony of flamingoes. People come to study them from all over Europe.'

'You know, I think you might actually have something there,' Chavasse said.

'More than that, my dear Paul, I have the

equipment to go with it. A small cabin-cruiser and all the extras I could think of. A rubber boat, shooting jackets and waders, binoculars, a decent camera. I checked with S2 in London and got the go-ahead. It seemed pointless to waste time.'

'Marvellous.' Chavasse was aware of a sudden irrational affection for him and clapped him on the shoulder. 'Truly marvellous.'

'No need to overdo it, Paul. For this kind of exercise I get a handsome fee – double if I assist in the field.'

'Do you want to?'

'I know the Camargue and you don't, so it would seem sensible.' He smiled. 'And you really have no idea how boring life is these days. A little action would definitely be good for my soul.'

'That's settled then.' Chavasse turned to Darcy, who was sitting in the rear. 'Nothing like some organization.'

'Oh, I'm impressed,' Darcy said. 'I'd be even more so if someone could remember to fill my belly within the next couple of hours. It's contracted so much it's beginning to hurt.'

'That, too, I have arranged, monsieur,' Malik said. 'My café is a stone's throw from the harbour. There my wife will reluctantly provide you with bouillabaisse, simply because it's the local speciality, but if you have sense, you will choose her stuffed mutton and rice and earn her eternal friendship.'

'Lead on, that's all I ask,' Darcy said, and Malik swung the Renault from one line of traffic to the next, narrowly missing a bus, and turned into a narrow street leading down to the harbour.

The stuffed mutton and fried rice was everything Malik had promised; after eating, they drove down to the old harbour, parked the Renault and walked along a stone jetty. There were boats of all shapes and sizes riding at anchor, and scores of dinghies and tenders of every description were tied close to the jetty. They went down the steps and Malik hauled in a six-man inflatable.

Chavasse did the rowing and, under orders, threaded his way through the crowded harbour until they fetched up alongside a twenty-foot fibreglass cabin-cruiser powered by an outboard motor. She was named *L'Alouette* and was painted white with scarlet trim. Darcy climbed aboard, then turned to give Malik a hand. Chavasse followed, after tying up the tender.

The cabin was small, the two padded side-benches making up into beds at night. The only other accommodation was a lavatory and a small galley.

Malik sat down with a sigh, produced a thin black cheroot and lit it. 'And now to business. You'll find a map in that locker, Paul, as well as a false bottom, under which are a couple of machine pistols and half-a-dozen grenades. It seemed like a good idea.'

The map unfolded to show the Camargue in detail; not only the several mouths of the Rhône, but every lagoon, every sandbank, every waterway.

'You can't go too much by this,' Malik said. 'The action of the tide, and the current from the river combine pretty forcefully. A sand-bank can be there one day and gone the next, and some of the waterways can silt up just as quickly. We shouldn't have too much trouble, though. *L'Alouette* only draws two or three feet.'

'And Hellgate? Have you managed to pinpoint it on the map?' Darcy asked.

'Indeed I have. See, just a little on the Marseille side of the Pointe du Nord. Three or four miles inland is the village of Chatillon. Hellgate is marked there, a couple of miles northeast of the village.'

Chavasse found it at once, an island in a lagoon that was shaped like a half-moon. 'Have you managed to find out anything of the place or Montefiore?'

'Naturally, I've been mainly restricted to Marseille because of the time element, but I've managed to produce some useful information. The house is about seventy years old. Built in the nineties by a Russian novelist called Kurbsky who didn't like the Czar and made it obvious. His novels had quite a vogue at the time in America and Europe generally, and he became a wealthy man. He came across the Camargue on a visit to a bull farm in the area and decided to stay. He had the house built where it was because he had an obsession with privacy. It's a wooden building and very Russian in style.'

'What happened to him?'

'He returned home after the Revolution – a grave error. He didn't like Lenin any more than he did the Czar, only this time he couldn't get out. He died in 1925, or was killed off. None of this required any genius, by the way. There is an excellent library in Marseille. I had a friend in the provincial land records office telephone through to Arles to see who owns the place now. It was used as a base by German troops during the war. Afterwards, it was empty until four years ago, when it was purchased by someone named Leduc.'

'Leduc?' Chavasse frowned.

'That was the name on the register.'

Chavasse nodded slowly. 'All right, I'd better fill you in on the details, then you know where you stand.'

When he had finished, Malik looked thoughtful. 'A strange business. This man Rossiter, for example. On the one hand, a bungling amateur who leaves himself wide open. On the other, a ruthless, cold-blooded killer without the slightest scruples.'

'And Ho Tsen?'

'Nasty – very nasty. What's a real pro doing mixed up with people like that?'

'That's what we've got to try and find out,' Chavasse said. 'Although I've got my own ideas on that subject. You know how difficult it is for the Chinese where espionage is concerned. The Russians don't have anything like the same trouble because they can pass off their own people as nationals of most other countries. The Chinese obviously can't do that, which explains why they're willing to use a man like Rossiter, amateur or no amateur. Mind you, that still doesn't explain how someone like Montefiore fits in.'

Malik nodded. 'And what happens afterwards?'

'Elimination – total and absolute.'

'And the girl,' Darcy put in. 'What about her?'

'If we can, we get her out.'

'But only if we can?'

206

'Exactly. Now let's get going. With most of the afternoon left, we can get a hell of a lot done before nightfall. Agreed, Jacob?'

Malik nodded. 'I'll take her out of the harbour. I know what I'm doing. With this engine, we should make it in a little over three hours, allowing for the weather of course, which I must say doesn't look too good.'

He went out on deck and Chavasse followed him. He stood at the rail, looking back at Marseille, as they moved out to sea. An old city – they had all been here. Phoenician, Greek, Roman. Beyond Cap Croisette, the sky was dark and ominous, and as they lifted to meet the swell from the open sea, rain spotted the deck in great heavy drops.

From the sea, the Camargue was a line of sand dunes drifting into the distance, and as they moved in, great banks of reeds and marsh grass lifted out of the water as if to greet them. With them came the heavy, pungent odour of the marshes, compounded of salt and rotting vegetation and black gaseous mud, a smell that

207

hinted at a darker, more primeval world, a place that time had bypassed.

The bad weather had not developed as expected and the rain had held off except for intermittent showers. As they moved in towards the land, Malik once more took the wheel and Chavasse and Darcy stood at the rail.

Half-a-dozen white horses stood on a sandbank and watched them as they went by, and beyond, hundreds of flamingoes paced through the shallows, setting the air aflame with the glory of their plumage.

'What happens now, Paul?' Malik asked. 'Do we stop at the village or keep going?'

'No harm in calling in,' Chavasse said. 'You can visit the local shop, see what you can find out. Darcy and I had better stay in the background, just in case.'

'All right,' Malik nodded. 'To pass *through* without stopping would probably engender an unhealthy interest about our identity and business anyway. Small communities are the same the world over.'

And Chatillon was certainly that: two primitive wooden jetties standing just out of the water, an assortment of small boats and a couple of dozen houses. Malik took *L'Alouette* to the extreme end of one of the jetties and Chavasse tied up. Darcy stayed below.

The Pole limped away and Chavasse lounged in the stern, fiddling with a fishing rod, part of the general equipment Malik had provided. There didn't seem to be a great deal of activity on shore. About fifty yards away a man worked on a boat, and two old men sat on the other jetty mending wildfowling nets.

Malik returned in fifteen minutes carrying a paper bag loaded with various provisions. 'Typical French provincials,' he said, as Chavasse helped him over the rail. 'Suspicious as hell of all strangers, but wanting to know every last detail of your business.'

'And what did you tell them?'

'That I was from Marseille with a friend to do some birdwatching and a little fishing. As I told you before, they get people like that in here all the time.'

'And they accepted your story?'

'Completely. It was an old woman in her seventies and her idiot son. I got out the map and asked her where there was a good place to tie up for the night, which gave me an excuse to put my finger on Hellgate amongst other places.'

'What was her reaction?'

'Nothing very exciting. It's private. Nice people, but they don't encourage visitors.'

'Fair enough,' Chavasse said. 'Let's get moving. It'll be dark soon.'

Thunder rumbled menacingly in the distance and Malik started the outboard as Chavasse cast off. Darcy didn't come on deck until they were well away from the village, moving along a narrow channel, reeds pressing in on either hand.

Chavasse scrambled up on top of the cabin and opened the map. At first it was relatively simple to chart a course, but it became progressively more difficult the deeper into the marshes they went.

They had deliberately avoided staying with the principal waterway that gave direct access to Hellgate and kept to the northeast, so that in the end, they were approaching it from the rear.

It was almost dark when they turned into a

small lagoon, and Chavasse called softly, 'Okay, we'll make this do.'

Malik cut the motor and Darcy heaved the anchor over the side into eight or nine feet of water. Suddenly, it was quiet, except for the croaking of bullfrogs and the occasional stirring of a bird in the thickets.

'How far?' Darcy asked.

'Quarter of a mile, no more,' Chavasse said. 'We'll go on in the rubber boat at first light and take a look at the place.'

'An interesting prospect,' Malik said.

'Oh, it should be that, all right.'

Above them thunder cracked the sky wide open and as darkness fell, rain fell with it in a sudden drenching downpour that sent them running to the shelter of the cabin.

# HELLGATE

# 13

It was a cold grey world that Chavasse stepped into when he went on deck at four-thirty the following morning. Rain hammered into the waters of the marsh with a thousand voices and yet life stirred out there in the gloom. Birds called and wild geese lifted into the rain.

He was wearing waterproof nylon waders, a hooded anorak, and a pair of binoculars hung around his neck. Darcy Preston joined him, wearing a similar outfit, and was followed by Malik, who sheltered under a large black umbrella.

'The last place God made.' The Pole shuddered. 'I'd forgotten there was such a time of day.'

'Good for the soul, Jacob.' Chavasse hauled

215

in the dinghy. 'We shouldn't be long – a couple of hours at the most. I just want to size things up, that's all.'

'Just make sure you know how to find your way back,' Malik said. 'It's not too easy in a place like this.'

Darcy Preston took the oars and pulled away and in a few moments *L'Alouette* had faded into the murk. Chavasse used the map and compass and charted a course for Hellgate that took them in a straight line through mud and reeds and narrow waterways, penetrating deeper and deeper into a lost world.

'This is how it must have seemed at the beginning of time,' Darcy said. 'Nothing's changed.'

There was a rustle in the reeds on their left; they parted, and a young bull ploughed through. He stopped in the shallows and watched them suspiciously.

'Just keep going,' Chavasse said. 'That's a fighting bull with a pedigree as long as your arm. They don't take kindly to strangers.'

Darcy pulled harder and the bull faded from view. 'I certainly wouldn't like to be on foot with one of those things on my tail,' he said.

'What in the name of good sense are they doing running around loose?'

'This is where they raise them. This is bull country, Darcy. They just about worship the damn things. We're the interlopers, not the bulls.'

They emerged into a large lagoon and the towers of the house loomed out of the mist fifty yards away. Chavasse made a quick gesture and Darcy pulled into the shelter of the reeds on the right. There was a patch of high ground beyond and they beached the dinghy and got out. Chavasse crouched and focused the binoculars.

As Malik had said, the house was very Russian in style and constructed of wood, with a four-storey tower at each end and a veranda at the front. The whole was surrounded by pine trees which had probably been specially planted when it was first built, but what had originally been the garden was now an overgrown jungle.

There was something curiously false about the place. It was too much like the real thing – a film set for a Hollywood version of a Chekhov play.

Chavasse couldn't see the landing stage, which presumably was on the other side. From an approach point of view, the house couldn't have had a better strategic situation. The lagoon was crescent-shaped and about a hundred yards wide and two hundred long. There was no possibility of an approach under cover during daylight.

He passed the binoculars to Darcy. 'What do you think?'

The Jamaican had a look and shook his head. 'I don't see how anyone could get any closer during daylight without being spotted.'

At that moment a dog barked and two men came running round the corner of the house. They jumped into view when Chavasse focused the binoculars – two Chinese, each clutching an assault rifle. The dog joined them a moment later, an Alsatian; it ran backwards and for-wards, rooting in the undergrowth.

'I don't know what it's looking for, but it won't get much of a scent in this rain, that's for certain,' Darcy said.

'I wouldn't be too sure.' Chavasse watched intently through the binoculars. 'It takes a lot to fool a German Shepherd.'

There was a sudden commotion over on the right, a heavy splashing as something forced its way through the reeds. At first Chavasse thought it might be another bull, but he pulled out the Walther PPK just in case. There was a groan of pain, then a splash followed by a cry for help in French.

Chavasse and Darcy pushed through the reeds and emerged on the other side of the sandbank, as a head broke the water in the channel beyond and a hand clutched feebly at air.

Chavasse plunged forward, the water reaching to his chest, and grabbed for the outstretched hand as the man went under again. Their fingers met and he went back slowly, the thick black bottom mud reluctant to let him go.

Darcy gave him a hand and they laid him on his back in the rain, a thin, grey-haired emaciated man of seventy or so. He wore pyjama trousers and a sleeveless vest and his body was blue with cold. His eyes rolled wildly, he gibbered with fear, then passed out.

'Poor devil.' Chavasse raised one stick-like arm. 'Ever seen anything like that before?'

Darcy examined the multiple tiny scars and

219

nodded soberly. 'A heroin addict by the look of it, and pretty far gone. I wonder who he is?'

Chavasse started to take off his anorak. 'Last time I saw him was in a photo Mallory showed me, though I must say he was looking considerably healthier.'

'Montefiore?' Darcy said blankly.

'In person.' Chavasse raised the unconscious man, slipped the anorak down over his head and picked him up. 'Now let's get out of here before he dies on us.'

On the return journey, Chavasse sat in the stern, Enrico Montefiore cradled in his arms. He was in a bad way, there was little doubt of that, and moaned restlessly, occasionally crying out, and yet never once did he regain consciousness.

There was the sound of the Alsatian barking uncomfortably close somewhere and then the harsh chatter of an outboard motor shattered the morning quiet.

Chavasse sat with the compass in his free hand, relaying precise instructions to Darcy, who was putting his back into the rowing. At one point they stuck in a particularly thick patch of reeds and he eased Montefiore to the floor and went over the side to push.

It was cold – bitterly cold, for by this time the water had managed to get inside his nylon waders, and without his anorak the upper part of his body had no protection at all.

The dog barked monotonously, much nearer now, the sound of the outboard motor coming in relentlessly. Chavasse pushed hard and scrambled aboard as the dinghy moved again.

A few moments later, they broke from cover and drifted into clear water and *L'Alouette* loomed out of the mist.

'Jacob!' Chavasse called and then, as they moved closer, saw that Malik was sitting in the stern, his black umbrella shielding him from the rain.

The dinghy bumped gently against the side of *L'Alouette*. Chavasse stood up and looked straight into Malik's face beneath the black umbrella, which he now realized was lashed to the stern rail with a length of rope. Malik's eyes were fixed in death, his left ear was missing and

there was a small blue hole just above the bridge
of his nose.

'Good morning, Chavasse, welcome aboard.'

Rossiter moved out of the cabin, smiling
pleasantly as if really delighted to be meeting
him again.

Colonel Ho Tsen stood in the background, one
side of his face covered in surgical tape. He
was holding an AK assault rife and looked
grim and implacable, every inch the professional.

'One of my men took a photo of you as you
came in last night,' Rossiter said. 'We always
like to check on new arrivals in this part of the
Camargue. You may imagine my surprise when
he showed me the print.'

'You took your time getting here,' Chavasse
said. 'You're not too efficient.'

'This wretched weather, old man. We got
here just after you left. So we decided to wait.
Actually, our time wasn't wasted. Your friend
was quite forthcoming after the colonel had a
few words with him. Oh, yes, I now realize that

you know all about us, Chavasse. On the other hand, we know all about you.'

'How nice for you. And what about Montefiore?'

'A problem. He's done this before, which simply isn't good enough. I must have a word with the person who was supposed to be looking after him.'

He went to the door, produced a whistle and blew three blasts. As he turned, Darcy Preston said harshly, 'Who put him on heroin – you?'

'It keeps him amenable most of the time,' Rossiter said.

'As a living vegetable. Why don't you let him die?'

'But who on earth would sign all the cheques?' Rossiter demanded in a half-humorous manner, as if trying to be reasonable about the whole thing.

Which explained a great deal. And then several things happened at once. Montefiore started to groan, thrashed his limbs wildly and sat up, and a dinghy powered by an outboard motor appeared from the mist carrying two Chinese men and the Alsatian.

The two men came aboard, leaving the dog in the dinghy. Ho Tsen spoke sharply to one of them in Chinese, so rapidly that Chavasse could not hear what was said. The man replied in a low voice, eyes down and Ho Tsen slapped him across the face.

'Have they got a dose with them?' Rossiter demanded in Chinese.

One of the men put down his assault rifle and produced a small leather case. He opened it, took out a hypodermic and a glass ampoule. Rossiter filled the hypo and nodded to the Chinese who held Montefiore down by the shoulders. Rossiter gave him the injection.

'That should hold him.'

Montefiore stopped struggling and went very still, all tenseness leaving him, and then a strange thing happened. His eyes opened and he looked up at Rossiter and smiled.

'Father Leonard?' he said. 'Father Leonard, is that you?'

And smiling, the breath went out of him in a quiet sigh and his head slipped to one side.

There was a sudden silence. Rossiter gently

touched his face. It was Ho Tsen who moved first. He pushed Rossiter out of the way and shook Montefiore roughly. Then he turned, his eyes angry.

'He's dead – do you understand? You've killed him. I warned you – I told you you were giving him too much.' He struck out at Rossiter, sending him back against the other bunk. 'One error after another. You'll have a lot to answer for when we reach Tirana.'

For a moment, all attention was focused on the Englishman. Chavasse sent the other Chinese staggering, turned and jumped for the door. He went over the rail, surfaced and struck out for the shelter of the reeds.

He threw a quick glance over his shoulder and saw Darcy struggling with the two Chinese at the rail. Ho Tsen appeared, clubbed the Jamaican with the butt of his rifle and raised it to his shoulder. As he started to fire, Chavasse went under the water and swam for the reeds.

Safely in their shelter, he turned and looked back. The two Chinese were already in the dinghy and casting off; the dog was howling like a wolf. Chavasse started to push through the reeds, half-swimming, half-wading. And then another sound rent the morning: the motor of *L'Alouette* as she got underway.

He came to a waterway so deep that his feet failed to touch bottom. He swam across to a grey-green wall of palm grass and forced his way through. He paused after a few minutes, treading water. The sound of *L'Alouette* was fading. Presumably it was heading for Hellgate, but the outboard motor of the dinghy was popping away in the vicinity and the Alsatian's mournful howl echoed eerily through the rain like a voice from the grave.

Chavasse started to swim again, pushing his way through the reeds; suddenly the sound of the outboard motor ceased abruptly and the dog stopped barking. Which wasn't good, whichever way you looked at it, because now he didn't have the slightest idea where they were.

His feet touched bottom, and he ploughed through thick black mud and moved out of reeds and grass to relatively firm ground. The compass still hung around his neck, enabling him to check his direction, and he concentrated hard, trying to recapture a pictorial image of the map. It was an old trick and surprisingly effective. The island would be the only one of any size in the vicinity of *L'Alouette*'s anchorage, a couple of hundred yards in diameter and a quarter of a mile southwest of Hellgate.

He started to run, then came to a dead stop as a bull loomed out of the mist to confront him. The animal held its head high and stared him right in the eye. Steam drifted from its nostrils and Chavasse backed away slowly. There was a movement to his right as another bull appeared like a dark shadow, flanks glistening. It pawed the ground nervously, its head dipped, the great curving horns gleaming viciously, and then another appeared beyond the first and yet another, six or seven of the great beasts in all, fighting bulls reared for their courage and heart, bred to fight in the ring.

He took a deep breath and walked through them very slowly, passing so close between two of the outer circle that he could have reached out and touched them. He kept on going, stumbling through tussocks of marsh grass, and emerged on a sandy shore. There was a sharp cry, followed by two shots close together, and sand fountained into the air on his right.

The dinghy drifted out of the mist perhaps twenty yards away. In a single frozen moment of time he saw clearly that the Alsatian was muzzled, but not for long. The AK assault rifle cracked again, and as Chavasse turned to run, the Alsatian took to the water.

He didn't have long – a minute or a minute and a half at the most before it ran him down. He tugged feverishly at his belt as he stumbled on. There was a technique for handling big dogs, but its successful application depended entirely on keeping calm and having a hell of a lot of luck in the first few seconds of attack.

The belt came free; he looped it around each hand, then turned and waited, holding his hands straight out in front of him, the belt taut.

The Alsatian came out of the mist on the run and skidded briefly to a halt. In almost the same moment, it moved in, mouth wide. Chavasse pushed the belt at it and the old trick worked like a charm. The Alsatian grabbed at it, teeth tearing at the leather. Chavasse jerked with all his strength, bringing the dog up on its hind legs and kicked it savagely in the loins.

The Alsatian rolled over and he kicked it again in the ribs and the head. It howled terribly, writhing in the mud, and he turned and moved on as the two Chinese arrived.

Another shot followed him, and from somewhere near at hand there was a roar of pain. *The bulls.* In the heat of the moment he had forgotten about the bulls. There was a sudden trampling and one of them appeared, blood streaming from a wound in the shoulder.

Chavasse dived for the shelter of a clump of reeds and dropped on his face as heavy bodies crashed through the mud. There was a cry of dismay, a shot was fired and someone screamed. When he raised his head, he saw an old bull lurch out of the rain, one of the Chinese hanging across his head, impaled on the right horn. The bull shook the man free and started to trample him.

There were two more shots somewhere in the mist and then a terrible cry. Chavasse had heard enough. He moved out of the reeds quickly and took to the water. A few moments later he reached another patch of dry land, checked his compass and started to move southwest towards Hellgate.

It took him the best part of an hour to reach the vantage point from which he and Darcy had viewed the house that morning. He crouched in the reeds and peered across the lagoon. If anything, the mist had thickened and everything was indistinct, ghostlike, more than ever like a sad Russian landscape.

By now *L'Alouette* would be tied up at the landing stage on the other side of the island at the rear of the house and if anything was to be done, it would have to be from here.

To his left, reeds marched out into the grey water, providing plenty of cover for perhaps half of the distance. The final approach would be in the open – no other way.

He was still wearing the nylon waders Malik had provided, and now he sat down and pulled them off. Underneath he was wearing a pair of trousers so wet that they clung to him like a second skin. He moved round towards the line of reeds and waded into the water, crouching low. For the first time since his jump for freedom on *L'Alouette*, he felt cold – really cold – and shivered uncontrollably as the water rose higher. And then his feet lost touch with the bottom and he started to swim.

He paused at the extreme end of the reeds and trod water. There was about fifty yards of clear water left to cover. He took a couple of deep breaths, sank under the surface and started to swim. When he sounded for air, he was halfway there: He surfaced as gently as possible, turned on his back to rest for a brief moment, then went under again.

In a very short time, his body scraped the black mud of the bottom as he neared the island. He came to the surface and floundered ashore into the shelter of a line of bushes.

He crouched there in the rain, sobbing for breath, then got to his feet and moved on cautiously through the derelict garden to the house. There was no sound, not a sign of life – nothing, and a strange kind of panic touched him. What if they had left? What if Rossiter had decided to get out while the going was good? And then Famia Nadeem appeared at the end of the overgrown path he was following.

She wore rubber boots to the knees and an old naval duffel coat, the hood pulled up. She was the same and yet not the same, in some strange way a different person. She walked on, hands thrust into the pockets of her coat, face serious. Chavasse waited till she was abreast of him, then reached out from the bushes and touched her shoulder.

Her expression was something to see. The eyes widened, the mouth opened as if she would cry out, and then she took a deep shuddering breath.

'I couldn't believe it when Rossiter said you were alive.'

'He's here? You've seen him?'

She nodded. 'They came back in the other boat about an hour ago with Mr Jones, though he isn't Mr Jones any more, is he?'

Chavasse put a hand on her shoulder. 'How bad has it been?'

'Bad?' She seemed almost surprised. 'That's

a relative term, I guess. But we mustn't stand here talking like this. You'll get pneumonia. Through those trees is a derelict summerhouse. Wait there. I'll bring some dry clothes, and then we'll decide what's to be done.'

She faded like a ghost and he stood watching her through the quiet rain, conscious of the stillness, drained of all strength. God knew what Rossiter had done to her, but she had been used harshly, must have been for such a profound change to have occurred so quickly.

The summerhouse reminded him of childhood. The roof leaked and half the floorboards were missing and he slumped down against the wall underneath the gaping window. He used to play in just such a place a thousand years ago.

He closed his eyes, tiredness flooding over him, and a board creaked. When he looked up, Rossiter stood in the doorway, Famia at his side.

Her face was calm, completely impassive, pure as a painting of a medieval Madonna.

# 14

The cellar into which two more Chinese guards pushed him was so dark that he had to pause for a couple of moments after the door was closed, waiting for his eyes to become accustomed to the gloom.

'Darcy, are you there?' he called softly.

'Over here, Paul.' There was a movement in the darkness and Chavasse reached out.

'What happened when I jumped the boat? Are you all right?'

'A knock on the head, that's all. What about you? I thought you'd be long gone.'

Chavasse told him. When he had finished, the Jamaican sighed. 'He certainly must have got through to that girl.'

Chavasse nodded. 'It doesn't make sense. She knows what happened on the *Leopard*.

How can she possibly believe anything he says?'

'There could be a very simple explanation,' Darcy pointed out.

'She's fallen in love with him, you mean?'

'Could be more than that. Might be one of these strong sexual attractions that some people have for each other. It's possible.'

'I suppose so. Immaterial now, anyway.' Chavasse moved through the darkness, hand outstretched until he touched the wall. 'Have you explored?'

'Not really. I was still unconscious when they first dumped me in here.'

Chavasse moved along the wall, feeling his way cautiously. He touched some kind of flat board, felt for the edge and pulled. It came away with a splintering crash and light flooded in.

The window was barred, the glass long since disappeared. It was at ground level and the view was confined to a section of what had once been the lawn stretching down to the landing stage which Chavasse had been unable to see from the other side of the island.

The landing stage had definitely seen better

days and half of it had decayed into the lagoon. The rest was occupied by a forty-foot sea-going launch which had obviously once been a motor torpedo-boat, and *L'Alouette*.

Four men passed by, carrying boxes between them, and went towards the launch. They certainly weren't Chinese, and Chavasse strained forward and managed to catch the odd word as they passed by.

'Albanian,' he whispered to Darcy. 'Which makes sense. Remember the incident on *L'Alouette* when Ho Tsen took a swing at Rossiter? He told him he'd have a lot to answer for when they reached Tirana.'

'The only European Communist nation to ally itself with Red China rather than Russia. It certainly explains a great deal.'

The men returned from the launch. A few minutes later they reappeared, carrying a couple of heavy travelling trunks. 'Looks as if somebody is moving house,' Darcy commented.

Chavasse nodded. 'Destination Albania. They've got to get out, now that we've been nosing around. They've no guarantee that others won't follow.'

'But why keep us in one piece?' Darcy said. 'I wouldn't have thought they'd want excess baggage.'

'But we aren't. I've had dealings with the Albanians before, and the Chinese. They'd love to have me back. And you might be useful, too. They can't tell until they've squeezed you dry.'

The bolt rattled in the door, it opened and the two Chinese appeared. One of them held a machine pistol threateningly, the other came forward, grabbed Chavasse and pushed him roughly outside. They locked the door and shoved him along the corridor.

They passed through a large entrance hall, mounted a flight of uncarpeted stairs and knocked on the first door. It was opened, after a slight delay, by Rossiter who was wearing a dressing-gown. He looked as if he had just pulled it on and was certainly naked to the waist. He tightened the cord and nodded.

'Bring him in.'

Beyond him another door stood open and Chavasse caught a glimpse of a bed, the covers ruffled and Famia stepping into her skirt in front of a mirror. Rossiter closed the door and turned.

'You do keep popping up, don't you? Of course, now we know what you are, it isn't really surprising.'

'What's happened to the man from Peking?' Chavasse asked. 'Doesn't he want to put his two cents' worth in?'

'Indeed he does, but at the moment he's busy packing. Thanks to you and your friend, we're obviously going to have to leave in something of a hurry.'

'For Albania.'

Rossiter smiled. 'You really are on the ball. They'll love you in Tirana.'

'And all points east?'

'Naturally.' Rossiter produced a cigarette case and offered him one. 'A friendly warning. The colonel will want a few words with you when he arrives. Don't get awkward. You saw what he did to your friend. He only asked him once, then started carving. Your man talked fifteen to the dozen when he had one ear gone. I would have thought you could have done better than him.'

'He was an old man,' Chavasse said. 'Trying to make a little extra money. There was no need to do that to him.'

Rossiter shrugged. 'All over the world, thousands of people die every day. You friend Malik was just one more. If his death helps our cause, then he lived and died to some purpose.'

'Word perfect,' Chavasse said. 'They must have done a good job on you back there at Nom Bek.'

'You just don't understand – your kind never does.' Rossiter was grave and serious. 'I was like you once, Chavasse, until I was helped to find a new answer, a truer answer, a new meaning for life.'

'So now it's all right to kill people, old men and women?'

'For the cause, don't you see that? What's one life more or less – mine or yours? We're all expendable. How many men have you killed in your career? Ten? Twenty?'

'I don't notch my gun, if that's what you mean,' Chavasse said, feeling strangely uneasy.

'Have you ever killed a woman?'

Chavasse's mouth went dry, and for a brief moment, a face floated to the surface, the face of a woman he would have preferred to forget.

Rossiter smiled, the strange, saintly face

touched with something very close to compassion. 'I thought so. The difference between us is only in kind. The first and most important lesson to learn is that it isn't what we do that is so important as why we do it. I serve a cause – freedom for every man, justice, equality. Can you say as much? What do you defend, Chavasse? Imperialism, capitalism, the Church, decay everywhere, the people crushed and strangled, unable to breathe. God, when I think of the years I spent serving corruption.'

'With all its faults I'd rather have my way than yours. How many have the Chinese butchered in Tibet in the last five years? Half a million, give or take a few, all for the sake of the cause.'

Rossiter looked slightly exasperated. 'You just don't see, do you? No one matters – no person or persons. We're working for tomorrow, Chavasse, not today.'

Which, significantly, was the exact opposite of the teachings of the creed which he had been raised and educated to serve. Chavasse knew now that he really was wasting his time, but kept probing.

JACK HIGGINS

'So anything goes, even feeding poor old Montefiore heroin?'

'I first met Enrico Montefiore when I returned to Europe after the Korean War was over. My superiors had sent me to Vienna because they had decided that I was in need of psychiatric treatment to overcome the effects of what they were pleased to call Chinese brainwashing. Montefiore had been on drugs for years. One evening we received a call from a private sanatorium where he was a patient. He was extremely ill, and thought he needed a confessor.'

'And you were sent?'

Rossiter nodded. 'The start of a fruitful friendship. He came to – how shall I put it – depend on me? When I finally decided to give up Holy Orders, I persuaded Montefiore that he needed quiet and isolation, so he bought this place, under an assumed name. He was badly in decline by then. I've had to look after him like a baby for the past three years.'

'In between assignments for your bosses in Peking.'

'Tirana, Chavasse, let's get it right. Albania has proved a very useful European foothold for

242

us. Of course the Chinese have found me invaluable, for obvious reasons. They're in rather a difficult position as a rule. An Englishman can pass as a Russian if he speaks the language, but what can a Chinese do?'

'There are plenty of Hong Kong and Malayan Chinese living in Britain these days.'

'Indexed and filed – probably checked regularly by MI6 or Special Branch. Much better to be there and yet not there, if you follow me.'

'Which is where your service for immigrants came in?'

'Exactly, only it wasn't my service – it was Jacaud's. There he was running these people across the Channel by the boatload. West Indian, Pakistani, African, Indian – it was perfectly reasonable to have the odd Hong Kong Chinese in there as well.'

It was a bright idea and Chavasse nodded. 'Full marks for using your wits. So Ho Tsen wasn't the first?'

'If I told you how many, you'd feel rather sick.'

He smiled cheerfully, and Chavasse shrugged.

'But no more. They're not going to be too
pleased about that when you get back to head-
quarters.'

'Oh, I don't know. It couldn't go on for
ever and I do have you, after all – a very
useful prize.'

There was nothing Chavasse could say that
would erase the faint, superior smile from
Rossiter's face, and then for some reason he
recalled his conversation with Father da Souza.

'I was almost forgetting – I've a message for
you.' He lied with complete conviction. 'From
da Souza.'

The effect was shattering. Rossiter seemed to
shrink visibly. 'Father da Souza?'

'That's right. He has a parish near the East
India Docks in London. When I wanted information about you, he seemed the obvious person to see.'

'How is he?' Rossiter's voice was a whisper.

'Fine. He asked me to let you know that there
isn't a day in which he doesn't remember you
in his prayers. He was rather particular that I
should tell you that.'

Rossiter's face had turned pale and he spoke

through clenched teeth. 'I don't need his prayers, do you understand? I never did and I never will.'

The bedroom door opened and Famia emerged. She was wearing a raincoat and headscarf and carried a small suitcase. She ignored Chavasse and spoke to Rossiter.

'I'm ready. Shall I take this down to the boat?'

For a brief moment they might have been alone, for all the attention they paid Chavasse, trapped by that curious intimacy that only belongs to people hopelessly in love with each other. For Chavasse, this was the most interesting discovery of all – that Rossiter obviously genuinely cared for the girl.

He put a hand on her arm and guided her to the door. 'Yes, you take your case down to the boat. We'll be along later.'

One of the guards opened the door. She looked through Chavasse briefly, her face blank as if he wasn't really there, and went out.

As the door closed Chavasse said calmly, 'What did you do? Put something in her tea?'

Rossiter swung round, the look on his face terrible to see. His hand dipped into his pocket and emerged clutching the Madonna. There was a sharp click and the blade jumped into view. Chavasse crouched, arms up, expecting an attack at any moment. The door opened and Ho Tsen entered.

'Trouble?' he enquired in Chinese.

Rossiter seemed at a loss for words, in some way a different person, the awkward pupil caught out and having to justify himself to the schoolmaster.

A look of contempt appeared on Ho Tsen's face. He walked towards Chavasse, hands behind his back, and kicked him in the stomach when he was close enough.

It was expertly done, the work of someone who knew his karate. Chavasse was able to appreciate that much at least before he keeled over.

He rolled around a couple of times and fetched up against the wall. He lay there concentrating on recovering his breath while the voices droned somewhere in the distance, indistinct, meaningless. The colonel's foot had not caught him in the crotch, where such a blow could have had a permanently crippling effect, but in the lower abdomen, obviously by design.

Chavasse had at least been able to tense his muscles to receive it, and although sick and sore, he was already capable of some kind of movement when the two Chinese guards picked him up.

He played it to the hilt, dragging his feet on the way out and groaning softly. They took him down the stairs, across the hall and descended to the basement. When they reached the cellar, they dropped him to the floor. The one who carried a machine pistol over his shoulder now unslung it, holding it ready in his hands while the other got out a key and unlocked the door.

The man with the machine pistol leaned down and grabbed Chavasse by the collar, pulling him to his feet. Chavasse drove the stiffened fingers of his left hand under the chin into the exposed throat, a killing blow when expertly delivered. The man didn't even choke, simply sagged to the floor like an old sack, dropping his weapon. Chavasse came to his feet and lifted his elbow into the face of the man behind. The surprised

Chinese gave a stifled cry and went backwards into the cell. A strong hand jerked the man around, and Darcy Preston hit him once in the stomach and twice on the jaw.

In the silence, Chavasse picked up the machine pistol and grinned. 'I'd say we're in business again.'

'What's next on the agenda?' Darcy asked.

Chavasse held up the machine pistol. 'Even with this, we don't stand much of a chance against Rossiter, Ho Tsen and those Albanians. If we could get on board *L'Alouette*, things could look a little different. Those hand grenades and the machine pistols Malik hid in the false bottom of that locker could more than even things up.'

'What about the girl?'

'She sold us out, didn't she? As a matter of interest, your hunch was right. She and Rossiter can't keep their hands off each other. As far as I'm concerned, she's had it.'

He cut off any further discussion by leading the way outside and trying the other end of the passage. The first stairs they came to had a door at the top, which was not locked. When

Chavasse opened it cautiously, he looked into the kitchen, a large, square room with a fire burning on an open hearth. At that moment another door opened and two of the Albanians entered. Chavasse closed the door gently, put a finger to his lips and they retreated. At the far end of the passage, more steps took them to a door long disused. Darcy wrestled with the rusted bolt and it finally opened to reveal a small walled garden that was as much a jungle as anything else. They went out through an archway at the far end and ran for the shelter of the trees.

They made it and kept on going, Chavasse in the lead, following one of the overgrown paths, the undergrowth pressing in so close on either side that it brushed against them.

Without warning, the path emptied into a clearing on the edge of the lagoon in which stood the ruins of a fake Greek temple. Famia Nadeem was standing there, staring up at the broken columns, hands in the pockets of her duffel coat.

She swung round, startled, and an expression of real alarm appeared on her face. Chavasse dropped the machine pistol and grabbed her cruelly, clamping a hand across her mouth.

'Listen to me, you silly little bitch. Your boyfriend is an agent of the Chinese Communist Government. He's responsible for the deaths of a great many people, including old Hamid and Mrs Campbell. Do you understand?'

She gazed at him, wide-eyed, and he took his hand away. Immediately she opened her mouth, a scream rising in her throat, and he struck her on the jaw with his clenched fist.

He lowered her to the ground and turned to Preston. 'Sling her over your shoulder and make for the landing stage. Get as close as you can and wait in the bushes.'

'What are you going to do?'

'Create a diversion. If I can draw them off it will give you time to board *L'Alouette* and get moving.'

'What about you?'

'I'll swim out from here and join you on your way past, and if I'm not there in time, don't start getting all heroic on me. Just get out of here.'

'You're in charge.'

The Jamaican picked up the girl, slung her

over one shoulder and moved away into the undergrowth. Chavasse retrieved the machine pistol and hurried back towards the house. He already had a plan of sorts. The house was wholly constructed of timber. With the right encouragement it should go up like a torch, and there was one obvious place to start.

He moved back through the tangled garden and entered the basement again. This time, when he cautiously opened the door at the top of the second flight of stairs, the kitchen was empty.

He went in, removed the glass chimney from the oil lamp on the table and scattered its contents across the floor. He made a brief search through the cupboards and found a half-full can of paraffin in one of them. He emptied it to good effect, then moved towards the fire. Behind him, the door opened and Colonel Ho Tsen entered.

If he was armed, it didn't show, and in any case the machine pistol already had him covered.

Ho Tsen actually smiled. 'No sporting chance, Mr Chavasse?'

251

'In a pig's eye,' Chavasse said. 'The Breton half of me's in charge at the moment and we always pay our debts. This is for Jacob Malik.'

The first burst caught Ho Tsen in the right shoulder, spinning him around, and the second shattered his spine, driving him out through the open door. As he fell, Chavasse picked a burning log from the hearth and tossed it into the centre of the room. There was a minor explosion and he only just made it to the cellar door, flames reaching out to engulf him.

As he went out through the garden, he could hear cries of alarm from the other side of the house, the Albanians from the sound of it, running to see what had gone wrong, just as he had hoped.

He gave it another minute, then ran for the trees. As he reached their shelter, *L'Alouette*'s motor burst into life. So Darcy had made it after all? Behind him there was a sudden crackling as flames exploded through the windows, blowing out the glass.

A bullet splintered the trees above his head and he swung round, emptying the machine pistol in a wild burst that sent the Albanian who had fired at him in headlong retreat round the corner of the house.

Chavasse ran, head down, and shots chased him through the undergrowth, slicing through the pine trees above his head. He burst from cover and plunged headlong into the lagoon as *L'Alouette* appeared round the point about fifty yards out.

As he started to swim, *L'Alouette* altered course towards him, slewing to a halt broadside on as Darcy spun the wheel and cut the motor.

The Jamaican ran for the rail and pulled Chavasse over with easy strength.

'Get going, for Christ's sake,' Chavasse gasped.

As Darcy vanished into the wheelhouse, a bullet ricocheted from the rail as the first Albanian arrived at the water's edge. Chavasse turned and saw Rossiter appear from the trees with the other three men. The outboard of *L'Alouette* roared, and Darcy took her away in a burst of speed, bullets chopping into her hull.

# 15

Once around the southern tip of the island they were out of the direct line of fire, and safe. The girl lay on her face near the stern rail where Darcy had dropped her. When Chavasse picked her up she groaned and her eyelashes fluttered.

He took her into the cabin, laid her gently down on one of the seats, then opened the map locker and removed the false bottom. He unbuttoned his wet shirt, stuffed the grenades inside for ease in carrying, picked up the two machine pistols and went on deck.

Darcy was giving the motor all it had and Chavasse shook his head. 'You're wasting your time. That MTB has four times our speed. We've got maybe five minutes to get ready for them, so throttle down.'

'What do we do?'

'Fight the best way we know how. First of all, I'll show you how to use one of these things.'

He went over the finer points of the machine pistol briefly, then quickly primed the grenades. 'I want them to go off in a hurry. Three seconds is all you've got from the moment you release the handle, and don't you forget it. You take three – I'll take three. You can carry them inside your shirt.'

He looked back through the mist to where smoke drifted sluggishly through the heavy rain. 'I shouldn't think there will be much of Hellgate left after that little lot has burned itself out. Cut the motor.'

Somewhere not too far away, the engines of the MTB roared like an angry lion. They had entered a smaller lagoon and *L'Alouette* moved broadside towards the entrance of the narrow waterway at the far end. She drifted to a halt, her prow in the reeds, and Chavasse nodded.

'This is as good a place as any. Now let's have the girl up here and I'll tell you what we do next.'

\* \* \*

Her speed considerably reduced in the narrow waterway, the MTB was moving slowly when she entered the small lagoon, and the Albanian stationed in the prow, sub-machine gun at the ready, saw *L'Alouette* and cried out.

The engines of the MTB died and she moved on, carried by her own momentum, drifting past the place where Darcy Preston stood waist-deep among the reeds, holding Famia securely, a hand clamped across her mouth.

Chavasse waited on the other side of the lagoon on a piece of relatively high ground, soft black sand surrounded by marsh grass. Two grenades lay on the ground beside him, another was ready in his hand.

He caught a glimpse of Rossiter's flaxen hair in the window of the wheelhouse and then the MTB was abreast. She was perhaps twenty or thirty feet away from him when he tossed the first grenade. It bounced on the stern deck, rolled into the water and exploded. The MTB rocked in the turbulence and there was a cry of alarm as the man in the prow went headfirst into the water.

On the other side of the lagoon, Darcy pushed

the girl away from him, took a grenade from inside his shirt, pulled the pin and tossed it. It had further to go than he had realized and fell short, sending a fountain of water skywards. As he took out another one, the girl screamed and flung herself on him just as he threw it. It fell into the water no more than fifteen feet away and the blast flattened the reeds and blew them both over.

Darcy surfaced, reaching for the girl, and found himself under heavy fire from two of the Albanians who crouched by the rail of the MTB with sub-machine guns. In the wheel-house Rossiter gave the engines full power and spun the wheel, and in the same instant, Chavasse's second grenade exploded under the boat, blowing most of the stern away and taking the propeller with it. The MTB shuddered and bucked like a live thing. As she slowed, Chavasse tossed his last grenade. It landed amidships and exploded with shattering force.

Rossiter was at that very moment emerging from the wheelhouse and the blast blew him into the water. The MTB heeled over, black smoke pouring from the engine hatch. Two of the Albanians still crouched at the rail, firing towards Darcy. Chavasse moved a few yards to one side, to a place where he could get a clear view, and drove them both over the side with a long burst from his machine pistol.

There was some kind of explosion in the engine room and flames burst through the hatch. The entire boat lurched to one side, rolled over and started to sink.

It was all over. In the sudden quiet the only sound was Famia's hysterical crying as she floundered through the shallows, trying to pull free from Darcy Preston's restraining hand.

Chavasse slung his machine pistol and swam towards them. When he was close enough to their side of the lagoon, he started to wade, reaching for the girl's left hand. She struggled fiercely, with a strength that was frightening in its power. For a moment, the three of them were caught in a mad tableau, Chavasse hanging on to one hand, Darcy Preston the other, at the same time trying to hold his machine pistol out of the water under the mistaken impression that it would cease to function if wet.

And then it happened, like something out of a nightmare. Out of the water, amongst the floating wreckage, Rossiter rose like some terrible phoenix, his clothes soaked in blood. That strange ascetic face was calm, devoid of all expression, the wet flaxen hair plastered into a skullcap.

The girl screamed his name, struggled violently and tried to plunge towards him. In the same moment, his right hand went back, there was a click and a flash of steel in flight.

Everything seemed to happen at once. The girl, still frantically trying to tear herself free, floundered across Chavasse's path and the knife buried itself in her heart, the ivory Madonna protruding from beneath her breasts.

Rossiter gave a terrible cry, reaching out towards her, and Darcy Preston emptied the machine pistol into him, driving him under the surface of the water.

Chavasse caught the girl as she swayed, a look of complete surprise on her face. He held her close to him and gently eased out the knife. In the same moment that it left her body, the life went out of her also. She hung for a moment on his left arm and then he released her and she sank from sight.

He turned and Darcy cried, 'Is this what we came for, this butcher's shop?'

He threw the machine pistol into the water, turned and waded through the shallows to *L'Alouette*. Chavasse went after him, and when he scrambled over the rail, Darcy was already in the wheelhouse.

The boat started to move, pushing its way through the narrow waterway, emerging a few moments later into the main channel. Beyond, through the rain, the smoke drifted up from Hellgate. Chavasse knelt there by the rail, very cold, trembling slightly, drained of all emotion.

And then he realized a strange thing – he was still clutching Rossiter's knife in his right hand. The channel widened as they moved through the estuary out to sea and he stared down at the ivory Madonna.

'And how many men have you killed in your career, Chavasse?'

The words seemed to whisper in his ear as if Rossiter himself had spoken. In a sudden gesture of repugnance, Chavasse flung the knife from him. It glinted once, then sank beneath a wave. Somewhere overhead geese called as they moved out to sea and he rose to his feet wearily and went to join Darcy in the wheelhouse.